D0924706

Pigeons and Princesses

James Reeves's words and Edward Ardizzone's drawings combine to bring to
life the world of magic and legend. These
five stories introduce characters such as
little Monday who loved trouble, the
King who learnt the hard way that there's
no place like home, and the stonemason
who made a bargain with an elf and came
to regret it. The author is well known as a
children's poet, and the artist is one of
today's most admired illustrators.

Pigeons
and
Princesses

James Reeves

Beaver Books

First published in 1956 by
William Heinemann, Limited, 15 Queen Street,
London W1X 8BE
This paperback edition published in 1976 by
The Hamlyn Publishing Group Limited
London · New York · Sydney · Toronto
Astronaut House, Feltham, Middlesex, England

© Copyright this edition James Reeves 1976
ISBN 0 600 37133 6

Printed in England by
Cox & Wyman, Limited, London, Reading and
Fakenham
Set in Baskerville
Line drawings by Edward Ardizzone
Cover illustration by Edward Ardizzone

This book is sold subject to the condition that it shall
not in any manner be lent, re-sold, hired or otherwise
circulated without the publisher's prior consent in
writing in any form of binding or cover other than that
in which it is published and without a similar condition
including this condition being imposed on the sub-
sequent purchaser. No part of the book may be re-
produced, stored in a retrieval system, or transmitted,
in any form or by any electronic, mechanical, photo-
copying or recording means, or otherwise, without the
publisher's prior consent in writing.

Contents

The Discontented King

I

THERE was once a King who ruled over a pleasant country full of green hills, blue rivers and little busy towns. He lived in a square stone castle of medium size with tall stone towers, which the sun shone on from morning till night.

All round the castle was a park full of stately trees, and under the trees ran the King's deer that he sometimes hunted. The room where the King sat and signed papers and fixed his great red seal to them was a high sunny room, very warm and comfortable, overlooking a rose-garden, and beyond the rose-garden he could see the green park. Just outside the window was a tall spreading elm tree in which the white pigeons sat all day and made sweet cooing music. The King had a red robe with silver flowers on it and a great black horse for riding on when he travelled about his country. But still he was not happy. He was a discontented King, and it did not make things any better that he could not tell exactly why he was discontented.

The Queen was beautiful and graceful. She was nearly always cheerful and had a good temper. She was gay, amusing, and very fond of the King. She did not sit all day long on a silk sofa eating sweets and fanning herself, but was active and liked making things. She made cushion-covers and pillow-cases and long trailing gowns and tall elegant head-dresses. She liked riding about in the park too; but best of all she liked putting on her oldest dress and going into the kitchen when the chief cook was away and baking pastries and pies and sweetmeats and little sugar-rolls with cherries on top. She did not of course always wear her oldest dress. She had a blue robe with gold flowers on it, and a white horse for travelling round the country with the King. With such a Queen as his wife, the King ought to have been happy, but he was not. He was a discontented King, and it did not make it any better that he could not tell exactly why he was discontented.

The King and Queen had one daughter, who was gay and happy like her mother, but was not so fond of sewing and cooking. Instead she liked sitting in her little room high up in one of the castle towers and gazing out over the green fields to where on clear days she could just see the sea. She did not do this all day. Sometimes she would read, and sometimes she would help her mother or father. Sometimes she would even help her mother when she went into the kitchen to cook; especially when she was baking the little sugar-rolls with cherries on top. Sometimes she was so happy that she sang like a blackbird. She had a green robe and a dappled grey pony for riding about the country on, beside her father and mother. With such a daughter for Princess, the King ought to have been happy, but he was not. He was a discontented King, and it did not make it any better that he did not exactly know why he was discontented.

One day the King was sitting alone in his special room. He had done his signing and sealing for the day and was looking out of the window across the green lawns. The white pigeons were cooing peacefully in the great elm tree. It was a beautiful day, but still he was not happy. The Queen was in the kitchen, making little square tarts with slices of orange in them; the Princess could be heard chirruping away like a blackbird as she combed her long yellow hair in her little room at the top of the tower. She looked out of the window from time to time, to where her father's black horse and her mother's white one and her own dappled grey pony were grazing in the big meadow.

In the kitchen the Queen had a feeling that the King was not very happy, so when she had put her little orange tarts in the oven, she went up to the Princess's room and asked her to come down and talk to the King. The Princess had by now finished combing her hair and had done it up in a gold net with small gold leaves round the edge of it. She stopped singing when her mother told her the King was not happy.

"Oh dear," she sighed, "is father not happy again?"

"I'm afraid not, my dear," said the Queen. "Let us go down and see if we can suggest something to cheer him up."

They went down to the King's room and sat down one on each side of him.

"It is a beautiful day," said the Queen. "Would you like to go hunting?"

"You go," said the King, not exactly rudely, for he was never rude to the Queen; but still he did not want to go hunting.

"Well, what about a game of draughts with the new set made of red and white ivory?" said the Princess. "I love playing draughts."

"Well, have a game with your mother," said the King, not exactly rudely, for he was never rude to the Princess; but still he did not want to play draughts.

"What about a swim in the lake?" said the Queen.

"Let the fishes swim," said the King. "It is what they are for."

"What about some music, Father?" suggested the Princess. "You know you love music, and you have not yet heard the three new trumpeters who have come from Bohemia to join the royal band."

"I have heard them practising all the morning," said the King. "Three trumpeters cannot practise in a castle like this without *everybody* hearing them. Not that they are not very good trumpeters, but when you feel as I do, the last thing you want to hear is a trumpet. I am tired of music. As a matter of fact," went on the King unhappily, "I am tired of everything. I am tired of hunting, I am tired of signing papers, I am tired of playing games, and I am tired of music and dancing and all the things I used to like best."

The Queen and the Princess both looked very sad and the Princess began to cry a little.

"Oh, my dears," said the King, sorry to see the

Princess's tears, "I am not tired of you. Oh, not at all. But I am tired of everything else. Listen to those silly pigeons cooing in that tree. I am tired of them. Above all I am tired of this castle."

"But it is a lovely castle," said the Queen, who was thinking of her orange tarts baking in the kitchen, and all the shining pots and pans on the shelves.

"It is a beautiful castle," said the Princess, who was thinking of her little room in the tower, where she kept all her books and her games and her clothes and the shining mirror and hairbrush and comb on her dressing-table.

The King got up and put one hand on the Queen's shoulder and the other hand on the Princess's.

"My dears," he said, "if you do not mind, we will leave this castle and find another one. The truth is, I am tired of it, and I shall not be happy as long as we are here. I am sorry if this distresses you, but it is the only thing to do. We shall go tomorrow, all three of us."

The Queen and the Princess did not like this idea, but they said nothing. They knew it was of no use to argue when the King was feeling like this.

"You, my dear," he said to the Queen, "may take your sewing-basket and your favourite lady-in-waiting and a little serving-maid to help you if you want to cook. And you," he said turning to the Princess, "may pack up some of your favourite belongings, and you shall have a room to yourself just like your own room here."

So it was arranged. The Queen agreed because she was a cheerful and contented person who usually did as the King wished. Besides she wanted to get back to the kitchen to see to her little square tarts—which indeed, were only just saved from burning. They were all to set off next morning. The Lord Chamberlain was to go on in front in order to take possession of any castle that the King might fancy and to turn out any people that might happen to be living there. He was to have a small army with him, just a few knights and men, in case of difficulty. It may not seem polite or kind to turn people out of their homes, but really most people are glad of a change, and it is considered an honour to have the King living in your house. That is why the army was a very small one. It was not thought likely that there would be any difficulty. The three trumpeters from Bohemia were also to go on ahead to announce the King's arrival.

The Queen took her waiting-lady and her serving-maid and some of her favourite things; and the Princess packed up her most treasured belongings, as the King had said. Next morning the King put on his red robe with the silver flowers on, and the Queen put on her robe of blue with the gold flowers, and the Princess put on her green robe. The King got up on his black horse, and the Queen got up on her white one, and the Princess got up on her dappled grey pony. The three trumpeters blew a cheerful blast on their three trumpets, and the Lord Chamberlain rode on ahead with the knights and men. The servants rode behind. It was a beautiful morning, and everyone chattered happily. As they went out of the gates into the park, the white pigeons were cooing gently and peacefully in the elm tree.

"Really," said the Queen, "this is not such a bad idea. Perhaps we all needed a change."

"I'm so excited," said the Princess. "This is quite an adventure."

And the King laughed and began to sing a little. This was so unusual that even the black horse wondered what had happened to his master. He neighed gladly, and so did the Queen's white horse and the Princess's dappled pony.

2

They rode on for two days, and on the third day the weather changed. It became cold and cloudy. They had reached the edge of the King's country and were now by the seashore. There was a big stone castle standing on the cliff just above the sea.

"This will do," said the King. "We will live here."

The Chamberlain went to the owner of the castle, who was an old man living there with his wife and only a very few servants. The old man and his wife were glad to move to a smaller house at the edge of their grounds. The three trumpeters blew a loud blast, and the King and Queen and all the others rode into the courtyard.

They soon made themselves comfortable. The King took as his state room a large hall overlooking the sea. The Queen had a pleasant room beside it, and was soon unpacking her sewing materials and other things with the help of her lady-in-waiting. The Princess had a big room in the tower. It was not unlike her own room at home, but it was much larger and instead of overlooking the green fields it overlooked the stone courtyard.

The Lord Chamberlain and the knights also found themselves rooms, and the three trumpeters were told to practise their trumpeting near the stables, as far away from the King as they could get.

For a month they all lived together in the castle by the sea. Everyone was contented, even the King. He had found new forests to hunt in. He even went out in a boat and fished. The Queen had soon found her way to the kitchen. It was not such a good kitchen as her own and nothing like so clean. However, she and the servants set to work and turned it out, and before long she was cooking there as well as she had ever done at home. The Princess at first missed her view over the green park, but from her window over the courtyard she could see people coming and going, and this amused her. She carolled away in her big room, or read her books, or went down the steep little path to the sea and played on the sands.

Then one day the Queen noticed that the King was looking miserable. She and the Princess went and talked to him.

"What is wrong, my dear?" asked the Queen.

"I don't know," said the King. "One thing is certain. We must move from this castle. I don't like it and it doesn't suit me."

"Is it the noise of the sea outside your window?" asked the Princess.

"Well, it's certainly very noisy," said the King.

"We could change your room," said the Queen, "and give you one on the other side."

"I don't think it's the noise of the sea altogether," said the King. "I just don't like the place. It's too large. Much too large. I ought to have known that to begin with. What on earth did you let me come to a great barracks of a place like this for?"

He was never exactly rude to the Queen, but this question was almost rude. He looked out of the window.

"There's something wrong with this place. I miss something, but I don't know what it is. At any rate I can't stay here a day longer."

The Queen and the Princess would cheerfully have stayed there for another six months, but they knew it was no use arguing.

By next morning everything was packed up once more and off they all went. The Lord Chamberlain and the trumpeters went first, with the knights and men-at-arms. Then came the King in his red robe with the silver flowers on it, riding his black horse; and the Queen in her blue robe with the gold flowers, riding her white horse; and the Princess in her green robe on her dappled grey pony. Everyone felt cheerful. As for the waiting-women and servants, they were always glad of a change.

They rode on for two days and on the third day

they came to a castle standing by the shore of a great blue lake.

"This will do," said the King, riding up to the Lord Chamberlain. "This is just what we want. Take it."

The castle was not difficult to take, for the owner was away, and the only people in it were three or four old servants, who did not at all mind having the royal family to live there.

Once more they settled down. The King had a room overlooking the lake, and the Queen found herself another beside it. The Princess had a little room at the top. It overlooked the lake and she could see the swans floating gracefully on its surface. True her room was dark and rather bare, but she made it as comfortable as she could and was soon singing away as she combed her yellow hair.

The King liked the new castle.

"It's a nice size," he said to the Queen. "That other place was much too big. Can't think how we ever lived there a day, much less a month."

The Queen agreed that the new castle was much smaller. The kitchen, indeed, was very small—too small if anything. There was scarcely room for all the pots and pans and jars and bowls and dishes and plates that a good kitchen must have. Still, she managed to make it more or less as she wanted, and was soon busy making some of the little sugar-rolls with cherries on top that the Princess loved so much.

"This place isn't going to be bad at all," said the Princess.

"Of course it isn't," said the King. "I told you it was just what we were looking for. Such a nice size—not too big and not too small."

Then he went down to a kind of pavilion by the

lake, took off his red robe with the silver flowers on it and his other royal robes, and put on a bathing costume. Soon he was swimming peacefully in the lake, while the swans glided round.

The weather was fine, and for a month everything went on well. Then the Queen again noticed that the King did not look altogether happy. She went and spoke to the Princess.

"I'm afraid this may mean another move," she said.

The King had indeed grown tired of swimming. He found the swans greedy and ill-tempered, beautiful as they were. He did not like playing draughts here any more than he had done at home. There was no creature in the neighbourhood worth hunting, and the noise of the three Bohemian trumpeters practising once more annoyed him.

He found the Queen in the kitchen.

"Why are you wearing that old dress?" he asked. "You look dreadful in it."

"Why, my love," said the Queen, much surprised, "you always say you like me best in this old dress, for then you know I am happy among my jars and dishes."

"Nonsense," said the King, not exactly rudely, for he never spoke to the Queen really rudely, but still he did not like her in her old cooking dress.

"Go and put on your blue robe with the gold flowers on it, for we must be moving."

"What, again?" asked the Queen, pretending to be surprised.

"You really want us to move again?" asked the Princess, who had just come in.

Yes, the King insisted on setting out once more.

and next morning, for the third time, off they went. The Lord Chamberlain went in front with the knights and trumpeters, then came the Queen in her blue robe with the gold flowers, riding her white horse; and the King in his red robe with the silver flowers, riding his black horse; and the Princess in her green robe, riding her grey pony. Then came the waiting-women and the servants, who were laughing and chatting merrily, for they never minded a move.

For two days they travelled like this, and on the third day the weather became terribly hot. The Princess sang no more, the Queen lost her cheerful looks, and even the horses began to pant and grumble. There was no more laughing and joking among the servants. They came to a great bare desert covered with stones, and at the edge of it there was a castle.

"This will do," said the King to the Lord Chamberlain. "Take it."

The Chamberlain said nothing, for he was much too hot to speak, and the trumpeters blew a feeble blast on their trumpets. In the castle lived a wicked knight with four fierce dogs, but the men-at-arms drove them out, and soon the King and his party were settled in the castle. The weather grew cooler. Everybody was soon happy again. The King and the knights rode their horses over the desert. The Queen embroidered a beautiful veil in her cool sewing room overlooking the garden. The Princess made herself comfortable in a little round room in a round tower at the top of the castle. The King had a handsome chamber over the main gateway, and there he would sit signing and sealing the important papers that came every day by a special messenger.

"Now this is not so bad," he said. "That other

place was really too small, and the one before was much too big, but this one is just right."

The Queen did not like to tell him that the kitchen was in such a state that she had not the heart to do any cooking. Instead, she went back to her embroidery.

But the cool weather did not last long. In another month it was just as hot as ever. Once more the King became unhappy. He looked out of the window of his great state-room. There was something missing, but he did not know what it was. He was much too unhappy to do anything.

"What a miserable place this is!" he said to the Queen and the Princess one day. "I really can't think how we ever came to settle here."

"Why, it's very comfortable," said the Princess,

who had grown to be quite content with the castle at the edge of the desert. "I have a lovely little room, and I can watch the queer creatures that come and play round the walls. My room is quite round, and I have never had a round room before."

The King took no notice, but said to the Queen: "Why are you always wearing your best robe nowadays? Why do I never see you in that homely old dress you use for cooking?"

The Queen did not like to tell him that she could do no cooking because the kitchen was so inconvenient, so she said nothing.

"All the same," said the King, "you'd better keep it on, for we must go travelling again. I really couldn't stay here another minute."

He was not exactly rude to the Queen, for he was never quite rude to her, but he spoke very sharply all the same.

Well, off they set once more in the hot, hot weather. The Lord Chamberlain went first, very hot in all his Chamberlain's robes, and the knights and the men-at-arms went with him. Then came the King in his red robe with the silver flowers, and the Queen in her blue robe with the gold flowers, and the Princess in her green robe, which she used for travelling about the kingdom. The King rode his black horse, and the Queen her white one, and the Princess her dappled grey pony. Then came the waiting-people and the servants, who were always glad of a change; they were not laughing and joking much, for the weather was terribly hot.

For two days they rode like this, and all the time the road ran uphill. The weather gradually became cooler, and this pleased the horses, which had grown very tired. Presently they came to mountainous country, and just beyond a thick fir-wood they saw a handsome castle looking across a valley to a great range of snow-mountains.

The King called the Lord Chamberlain to him.

"Will it do, Your Majesty?" asked the Lord Chamberlain.

"It will," answered the King. "Take it."

3

The castle in the mountains belonged to a knight who was away at the wars, and his lady was glad to leave it and go and live with her parents for a time, as she had become very lonely. So the three Bohemian trumpeters, who had grown skilful after all their months of practice, blew a splendid blast on their trumpets, and everyone rode into the courtyard.

"Now this is something like," said the King. He chose himself a noble room on the first floor, and the Queen had a fine sitting-room beside it. The Princess once more climbed to the top of the castle, where she found herself a little room with a view towards the snow-mountains. They all settled down and life began once more. The Queen did not find things easy, for she had no more material for sewing. She had used it all up. The kitchen was small and there was no room for her as well as the cook who prepared the ordinary meals. The Princess had read all her books. The trumpeters practised no more, for they had become so skilful that they needed no more practice for the time being. The Queen and the Princess took to playing draughts with each other to pass the time away. They became used to the new life, and soon the Princess was chirping away as merrily as ever. The King went hunting wolves in the great black forest at the castle gates.

"A much better place than that dreadful old wicked knight's castle at the edge of the desert," he said. "And a lot better than those other two castles we tried."

And they all agreed with him and hoped they would stay there some time.

Then it began to snow. Soon no more messengers could reach them because of the snow, so that the King had no papers to sign and seal. He had nothing at all to do, for there was no more hunting, and he was forced to join the knights and the men-at-arms in games of snowballing in the castle grounds. They snowballed each other in order to keep warm, for the weather continued very cold.

At the end of a month the Queen once more noticed that the King was looking unhappy. He was sitting in his state room muffled up in his red robe with the silver flowers on it, and several other robes, one of them of fur, on top of it. He was looking discontentedly out of the window at the great black pine trees with their snow-laden branches. He felt that he ought to be happy. Yet there was something missing, though he could not tell what it was. He had often said he had too much work to do, and now he had none. All the same, he was unhappy.

"Of all the castles we have lived in," said the King, "this is the worst. What is the good, I ask you, of being stuck away in a place like this, where nobody visits us unless it is a lost wolf in search of a dead rat or a starving bird? The castle by the sea was bad enough, but it was better than this. So was the one by the lake, and so was the one by the desert. That one was at least warm, but this is cold, cold, cold!"

The Queen said nothing. She and the waiting-woman had already packed up their belongings and were ready to go.

"And *draughty*!" the King went on. "In all my life I have never lived in so draughty a place. Listen to the wind howling up and down these miserable cold passages. I can't stay here another minute—not another minute!"

"This time," said the Queen, "I really think we ought to go home. We've tried four castles already, and you haven't liked any of them."

"Just as you like," said the King. "I don't care where we go so long as we get out of this draughty old ruin!"

"Hadn't we better wait till the snow melts and the weather's a bit warmer?" said the Queen.

"Certainly not. It will probably never melt. We must go at once, do you hear—at once!"

It was no use arguing. Once more everything was packed up, and they all set out. The King's red robe with the silver flowers was covered with a black fur cloak, and the Queen's blue robe with the gold flowers was covered with a brown fur cloak, and the Princesses green robe was covered with a white fur cloak. But how cold they all were! When they had gone a mile or two, the poor Princess was nearly weeping with the cold. The Queen was very sorry the King had made them all set off while the weather was cold, but she said nothing. Only she was determined that once they got home, nothing would make her leave it again in a hurry. Everyone was cold, and nobody chattered and laughed. The Chamberlain whistled to keep his spirits up, until the King told him to stop. The King was in a very bad temper. He was angry with the weather for being so cold, he was angry with the Queen for having allowed him to set out in such weather, and he was angry with himself for being so headstrong and discontented.

After some hours the wind blew stronger, and more snow began to fall. A terrible storm broke over them. They could no longer see which way they were going. They stumbled on as best they could. It was by now night time, and the moon, which ought to have been shining, was lost in the black storm. It was as much as they could do to keep together. The Princess was now crying piteously. There was nothing to do but struggle on. How the snow fell! How the wolves howled among the trees! How the wind blew in their faces and stung their cheeks!

"What a fool I have been!" said the King to himself. "Why did I ever allow myself to leave home with my dear Queen and the poor little Princess? We shall never reach home alive, and it will all be my fault."

But in the end, when they were tired out, and the horses could hardly go another step, the storm calmed down. The road had been going down hill steadily, and the weather became warmer. Although they did not know where they were, they knew they must be out of the mountains. When daylight came, they were in the middle of a thick mist. There was nothing to do but to go on until the mist cleared.

At last, in the middle of some open country dotted with trees, they saw a huge shape towering out of the mist. It was a castle. They could just make out its square shape and pointed towers. Everyone stopped.

"It will do," said the King in a tired voice to the Chamberlain. "Take it."

Three blasts were sounded on the three trumpets, and the Chamberlain and the knights and men-at-arms rode forward through the mist.

Presently the Chamberlain came back to where the King sat on his horse waiting. He told the King that the castle had been left by its owners and was now in the hands of robbers.

"What a careless fellow the owner must be to leave his castle like that!" said the King. "Send in the men-at-arms and turn the robbers out."

The knights and the men-at-arms made short work of the robbers. After half an hour's fighting the leader of the men-at-arms came out and told the King that the robbers had been driven off and were now lost in the mist. Once more the three trumpeters sounded their trumpets, and the royal party rode through the castle gateway. Then the mist began to clear. But already the Queen had recognised her home.

Yes, it was really their old home. They had come upon it in the mist without at first knowing it. Here they were at last, half dead with hunger and tired out, at the very gates of their own castle.

But what a mess the robbers had left! Everything was dirty and neglected. The furniture had not been polished, windows had been broken and not mended, nothing had been cleaned or washed for months.

After everybody had had a meal and a rest, the servants set to work and made the place as tidy and comfortable as possible, and it was not long before the King and the Queen and the Princess settled down to enjoy being at home again.

The Queen began to make cakes in her own kitchen, and to embroider and sew as she used to; the Princess was overjoyed to have her own little room in the tower overlooking the green park, and soon she was singing away and combing her hair as if she had never been away for a day, let alone several months.

As for the King, a whole pile of important papers arrived that very evening, and all these needed signing and sealing, so that he had work for a week. After all, he thought, as he sat down to his table and began work, home was not so bad, and all he had wanted was a little change. Then he looked up and listened to something he could hear outside the high window. The sun was shining. Far away in the meadow his own black horse and the Queen's white one and the Princess's dappled grey pony were feeding contentedly. Near at hand, the great elm tree spread its shady branches over the garden. The sound that had caught the King's ear was the cooing of the white pigeons in its leaves. What a peaceful, contented sound it was! That was what had been missing in all the other castles he had been to. There had been no cooing pigeons in the castle by the sea, or the castle by the lake, or the castle beside the desert, or the castle in the mountains. No, only in his own castle could he hear the peaceful noise of these contented birds. How wrong he had been to think the noise silly! It was the pleasantest noise in all the world, except for two—one was the talking of the Queen, who was nearly always good-humoured and cheerful, and the other was the singing of his little Princess as she combed her hair in the room upstairs in the tower.

When he had finished his work for the day, he sent for the Princess and asked her to play a game of draughts with him, and the Queen brought in some fresh orange tarts and some sugar-rolls with cherries on top. It was the happiest time they had spent since the King made them all set out on their long journey.

The Old Woman and the Four Noises

I

THERE was once an old woman living by herself in a little cottage. She was poor, but she had just enough money to live on, so long as she was careful. She worked hard, getting her meals ready, cleaning the floors and the pots and pans, and keeping her clothes neat and tidy. If she was ill, as sometimes she was, she had kind neighbours who did the shopping for her in the village, and cooked and cleaned for her till she was well again.

Her cottage was small, very small indeed. In fact, there were only two rooms—a kitchen and a living-room. She did not mind this at all. "The smaller the house, the sooner it's cleaned," she would say. Besides, what did she want with big rooms? There was a neat, warm stove in the living-room, with a hearth rug in front of it; beside the hearth rug there was a comfortable rocking-chair, where she would rest and read her newspaper till it was time for bed. There was a table and three chairs, a dresser for her plates and cups, and a few pictures on the walls. In one corner, away from the window, was her bed, for she had no separate bedroom. She liked to have her bed in the living-room. "For," said she, "bedrooms are always cold and often damp." So she was glad she had no bedroom. The windows of her living-room were low and small, but they looked out over the green fields where the cows and horses fed. There were green curtains with bunches of red roses on them.

The old woman kept no cat or dog, and she was not very often visited by neighbours and relatives; but she was quite content living alone in her cottage in the company of her pictures and dishes and chairs and all the things she loved.

Now in any house there are always certain noises, and the old woman's cottage had its own special noises. When anyone came in at the door, there was a long, high "Squea-eak!" It was always the same, just like that, a high "Squea-eak!" and whenever she heard it, the old woman knew that the front door was opening. However carefully you opened the door, and however softly you let fall the latch, the hinges always made the same high-squeaking sound.

Then just inside the door there was a floor-board that seemed to say "Creak, creak!" every time it was stepped on. "Creak, creak!" the board would say when anyone came in at the door and stepped upon it.

If there was a little wind, one of the low windows in the living-room would make a rattling sound—not very loud, but just loud enough for you to know it was there, "Rat-tattle, rat-tattle!" the window would say. "Rat-tattle, rat-tattle!"

But the squeaking of the door, and the creaking of the floor and the rattling of the window were not the only sounds to be heard in the old woman's cottage. There was one more, and this was made not by the cottage itself but by something that lived in it. This was a little mouse that had its hole in a warm and secret corner beside the hearth. The old woman had never seen the mouse, and it never came out in the daytime, but she knew it was there; for sometimes at night, when she had settled down in bed and had not quite gone to sleep, she would hear a little pattering. "Patter-patter," she would hear. "Patter-patter!" And if any crumbs had been left on the floor, they would certainly have gone by the morning. Sometimes the old woman would leave a few crumbs on purpose, though she knew she ought not, for mice were not supposed to be in the house. "Nasty, dirty creatures!" people would say. But the old woman was fond of her mouse, though she never saw it, and could not believe that it was a nasty, dirty creature. She was always glad to hear the noise of its little pattering feet before she settled down to sleep. "There's my little mouse," she would say sleepily, as if it were quite an old friend. The window would rattle quietly if there was a wind; and in the morning, when she went to fetch the milk from the doorstep, she would tread on the creaking board and open the door. "Creak-creak!" the floor would say, and "Squea-eak!" the door would say, as if they were both wishing her good morning.

The old woman did not think about the little noises

her cottage made. If she had been asked what sounds she liked best, she would probably have said "The birds singing and the church bells on Sundays and the noise of the brass band from the village when it passes my door once a month on its way to town." All the same, she would have missed her own particular little sounds if she had not heard them.

The nearest neighbour to the old woman was an old man, a carpenter who lived with his wife in the cottage next door. The carpenter was kind to the old woman, and helped her with some of the things she could not do for herself. One day he put up a shelf that had fallen down in the kitchen and another day he made her table stronger, so that it did not wobble when she had to cut a piece of extra tough meat. The carpenter had a little shed at the bottom of his garden, where he did his work and kept his tools— saws and planes and hammers and screwdrivers and chisels and all the things that carpenters need for their work.

2

One day it was very cold, and the old woman was pleased to see her good neighbour the carpenter coming down her path and past the window carrying a bundle of firewood. "Rat-tattle!" went the window, for there was a cold wind blowing; and "Creak-creak!" went the floorboard, as the old woman hurried to open the door; and "Squea-eak!" went the door as she opened it to the carpenter. He gave her the sticks and she thanked him. Then he said that, as it was such cold weather, he would bring her some logs next day for her fire. The old woman thanked him and asked what she could do in return, for she did not like to take favours for nothing.

"Well," said the carpenter, "if I bring you some thick wool, you may make me a pair of warm socks, for my wife, though she is a good woman, is a poor hand at knitting."

The old woman agreed to this, and next day about the same time she saw the carpenter passing her window with a wheelbarrow, and in the wheelbarrow were logs for her fire. She opened the door, and the carpenter began to bring in the logs, four at a time, and pile them up beside her stove to get warm and dry. As he did so, he heard the floor creak. Every time he passed over the board, it seemed to say "Creak-creak. Creak-creak!"

"There's a nasty creak in that floor-board," said the carpenter. "You must let me come and settle it with a couple of nails and a hammer."

"Oh, you mustn't trouble yourself," said the old woman. "I'm so used to it that I hardly notice it."

"No trouble at all," said the carpenter. "It won't take me a couple of minutes. Another thing," he continued, "that door of your squeaks. Nasty, weaselly squeak that has. I've noticed it before. Better let me bring an oil-can and settle that squeak while I'm about it."

Just then there was a gust of wind, and the window rattled. "Rat-tattle, rat-tattle!" went the window, and the carpenter said:

"Why deary me, now there's a worrying sort of noise for a body to have to listen to, day in day out. Now, I'll just fetch a screwdriver and tighten up them hinges, and you'll never hear it again."

34

"That's very good of you, neighbour, I'm sure," said the old woman, "and thank you kindly."

She did not really want the carpenter to settle all the noises, but what was she to say? He was such a very kind man, and liked to take trouble doing things for her.

The carpenter had now piled up all the logs beside the stove. He was just going when he saw a little dark hole in one corner.

"Hello," said he. "That looks like mice to me. Are there mice here, do you know?"

"Why yes, I think there are," said the old woman, "but they don't trouble me."

"Nasty, dirty creatures, mice. That's what they are," answered the carpenter. "Just you let me bring one of my traps and I'll soon settle *them*!"

The old woman was just going to say she didn't really want to trouble him to set a mouse-trap, when the carpenter strode to the door and went out, saying he would call the day after tomorrow to settle all the old woman's noises.

That night the old woman heard the sound of the little mouse, patter-patter on the floor, and she trembled to think of it caught in a cruel trap; and next day, when she heard the rattle of the window and the creak of the floor-board and the long, high squeak of the front door, they seemed to her friendly noises, and she thought she would miss them when the carpenter had called to settle them.

"Well," she said to herself. "I'm an old silly, that's what I am. Of course my neighbour is right. He is a very clever man and he ought to know. They *are* tiresome little noises when you come to think of it, and I daresay the cottage will be a nicer place without them."

3

The next day was colder than ever, and the old woman woke up not feeling at all well and coughing a little. She decided not to go out, as the wind was so cold; and indeed, the little window was rattling away as if it would fall off its hinges.

When the carpenter came with his tool-bag to get rid of the noises, as he had said he would, he noticed that the old woman was not looking well.

"I'll leave this little job till to-morrow," he said, "and send my wife round to comfort you, for it looks to me as if you ought to be in bed."

Presently the carpenter's wife came round, and helped the old woman to bed. Then she got her some hot food and said she would attend to the shopping and do a bit of cleaning and see that the old woman did not have to get out of bed.

All day the old woman lay in bed. She was not very ill, and by the evening she began to feel better. She thought she would be able to get up the next day. But although she was not very ill, she was worried. There was something on her mind. Then she remembered that if she was well, the carpenter would call next day and get rid of all her little cottage noises and set a cruel trap for the little mouse. She told herself she was silly to worry about it, and yet she couldn't help worrying.

And as she lay in bed, suddenly it seemed as if she heard a noise of little feet. It was not the mouse's feet, but something heavier. Then there was the sound of a small squeaky voice, just like some other sound that she knew well.

"Old woman, old woman," said the squeaky voice. "Are you awake?"

The old woman was not frightened, for it was a small voice and quite friendly. Then she remembered what the squeaky voice reminded her of. Of course! It was the voice of the door.

"Who are you?" asked the old woman.

"Don't be afraid," said the voice. "I am an elf. You cannot see me, but I live in your front door and I bring you luck. Every time the door is opened or closed, I squeak just to remind you I am here."

"Well, what an odd thing," said the old woman. "I never knew before that there was such a thing as a door-elf that squeaked, but now I come to think about it, I see no reason why there shouldn't be. Won't you come in and make yourself at home?"

"I *am* in," said the door-elf, "and I *am* at home. I want to have a little talk with you."

So the door-elf told the old woman that he knew all about the carpenter, and how he was coming to oil the hinges next day, so that the little door-elf would never again be able to live in the door.

"That's pretty serious," said the elf, "and I do hope you'll ask him please not to do anything of the kind, but to keep his oil for other things."

The old woman was just going to answer that she didn't know what to do, when there was another pattering of feet. This time a creaky little voice spoke.

"Hallo, old woman," said the creaky voice. "Are you awake?"

"Yes," said the old woman. "Who are you?"

"I am the floor-elf," said the creaky voice, "and I live in one of your floor-boards and every time somebody steps over me I creak just to remind you

37

I am here. I want to have a little talk with you."

"Certainly," said the old woman. "Come in and make yourself at home."

"I *am* in," said the little creaky voice, "and I *am* at home."

He too went on to tell the old women how he knew all about the carpenter and his hammer and his two nails, and how if she allowed him to hammer down the floor-board, the floor-elf would have nowhere to live and would never come back.

The old woman was just wondering what to say, when she heard the sound of more little feet, and this time a rattly voice spoke.

"Are you awake, old woman?" said the rattly voice. "I am the window-elf and I live in your window, and every time the wind blows I rattle just to show that I am here. I bring you good luck and scare away bad luck that tries to come in at the window. I want to have a little talk with you, old woman."

"Certainly," said the old woman. "Come in and make yourself at home."

"I *am* in," said the voice of the window-elf," and I *am* at home."

Then the rattly voice of the window-elf also went on to say how he had heard all about the carpenter with his screws and his screwdriver, and how he was coming next day to fasten the window tight so that it would rattle no more and the little window-elf would have to go away and never come back any more.

The old woman was just going to answer that she would see what could be done about it, when there was yet another sound. This time it was the very small pattering feet of the mouse. The old woman was surprised to hear the mouse speak in a tiny quavery voice.

"Hallo, old woman," said the mouse. "Don't be afraid, and don't be surprised that I can speak. All animals can talk when there's something really important to talk about. And I have something very important to talk about to-night."

"Welcome, mouse," said the old woman. "Come in and make yourself at home."

"I am in already," said the mouse, "and I always make myself at home. Thank you for the crumbs you put out last night."

"Oh dear," said the old woman. "That reminds me, I have been in bed all day and have put out nothing for you to-night and it is a very cold night for a mouse to go hungry in."

"Never mind," said the mouse. "If you don't object, I will just step into the larder and help myself to a little cheddar cheese and two crumbs of brown bread."

"All right," said the old woman. "But wouldn't it be better if you *all* had something to eat? Come along, boys—and mouse—suppose you all sit up at the table and have some supper. I'm afraid there is not much in the larder, but what there is you are welcome to."

The three elves thanked the old woman in their squeaky, creaky and rattly voices, and began to help themselves. There was the sound of clinking dishes and presently the supper began. The elves explained that they were all sitting *on* the table, because they were too small to sit on the chairs. The mouse, meanwhile, told her that he also had heard about the carpenter and his mouse-trap and how it would

39

frighten him away so that he would never be able to come again with his little pattering feet at night.

Just then the moon came out from behind a cloud and shone through the window of the cottage on to the table. And by its light the old woman saw the little mouse and the three elves. There they were, with their pointed caps and pointed shoes eating cheese and bread and pickles and a little cold sausage.

While she watched the supper party by the light of the moon, the old woman wondered what to do. She did not want the carpenter to come and settle things so that the elves and the little mouse could never come back again. But how could she stop him? If she told him what she had seen, he would just think her silly. She was sure he would not believe her story about the elves. So she looked up at the moon, and the moon seemed to be talking to her and telling her what to do. She watched it attentively for a few minutes, and then all at once it disappeared behind another cloud and the room was again in darkness.

"Hallo, elves and mouse," she called, "are you still there?"

"Yes, old woman," said the floor-elf in his creaky voice. "We are still here and have just finished supper. A very good supper it was too."

"Well, listen to me," said the old woman, "and I'll tell you what to do. To-morrow my neighbour the carpenter is coming to get rid of you with his oil-can and his hammer and two nails and his screwdriver and his mouse-trap."

"Yes, we know," they said. "Can't you tell him not to? You *do* want us to stay, don't you?"

"Yes, truly," said the old woman. "But it's no use my telling him not to get rid of you, for he is a very clever man and is sure to do it just the same. Now I will tell you what you must do. You must hide, do you understand? You must hide just for to-morrow. After that you can go back to your proper places."

"That's all very well," said the mouse. "But what about me? I am always hiding. He'll set his trap just the same."

"You must leave that to me, mouse," said the old woman. "I'll see that no harm comes to you."

So they all agreed to do as they were told. The door-elf went and hid in a cupboard in the kitchen, where the carpenter would never find him; the floor-elf hid behind the old woman's bed in the corner of the room; and the window-elf hid in the old dresser that stood against the wall. As for the little mouse, he said good-night to the three elves and the old woman and ran back to his hole behind the stove. After that, the old woman felt much happier and was soon sound asleep.

4

In the morning she was quite better. She listened to hear if the window was rattling, but there was no sound. Then she went quickly to the place where the floor creaked and walked over it several times, but not a sound was to be heard. Then she went to the door and opened it, but there was never a squeak. So she knew the three elves were still hiding. She got her breakfast and when she had finished it she washed the dishes and began sweeping the floor. No sooner had she started to do this than there was a knock at the door and the carpenter appeared with his bag of tools.

"Good morning," said he. "I am glad to see you up and better. Now I think we can settle these little noises of yours. Nasty, worrying noises they are too, but it won't take me long to get rid of them. Here we are! Oil-can for the door, hammer and two nails for the floor, screwdriver for the window, and—let me see, what was it? Yes, of course—mouse-trap for the little fellow behind the stove."

"That's very kind of you, I'm sure," said the old woman. "But you know, neighbour, I think we must have been mistaken. When I opened the door just now to let you in, I could hear no squeak—no squeak at all. Just you try it."

So the carpenter tried the door, and it was just as the old woman had said. There was no squeak, no squeak at all.

"Funny," says he, "very funny indeed. I could have sworn there was a squeak to that door when last I came here. Still, I'll just put a drop of oil on her hinges to make sure."

"No, no!" said the old woman. "Don't do that. Don't waste your oil on a pair of old hinges with no squeak to them. But if you could just put a drop on my big scissors, I'm sure they'd work easier."

So the carpenter did as he was asked and left the door alone. Then he began to look for the creaking board. He stood on the board where the creak had been before, but now there was never a creak.

"Funny," said he, "very funny indeed. I could have sworn there was a creak to that board last time I stood on her. Well, she's a bit loose, so perhaps I'd best put a couple of nails in her to make sure."

"No, no!" said the old woman. "Don't waste your nails on an old board that has no creak to her. Perhaps you could put one in the rocker of my chair, though, for it's getting very loose, and I'm afraid it may come right off."

So the carpenter did as he was asked, and when he had finished he looked for the rattling window. But of course the same thing happened again, for the window-elf, like the other two elves, was hiding.

"Funny," said he, "very funny indeed. I could have sworn there was a rattle to that window last time I was here. Perhaps I'd best tighten up her screws just so as to make sure."

"No, no!" said the old woman. "Don't waste your time on an old window that has no rattle to her. But if you could just tighten up the screw in my pair of coal-tongs, that would be really kind."

So the carpenter tightened up the screw in the coal-tongs, and then he got out his mouse-trap. He set it very carefully and put it down on the floor beside the little mouse's dark hole.

"There," he said. "I think that'll settle *him* all right."

"Thank you very much indeed, neighbour carpenter," said the old woman. "Now if you'd like a cup of tea, there's a kettle on the boil here and it won't take me two minutes to make it."

"Thank you kindly," said the carpenter, "but I must be getting on my way. I've brought the wool for my thick socks, if you've time to make them for me; for although my old woman is a great hand at a game of cards or reading bits of the newspaper, she's never been much of a one for plain knitting."

So the old woman took the wool and said she would gladly knit the socks. The carpenter took up his tool bag and left the cottage; and as he went, there was never a rattle from the window, nor a creak from the floor-board, nor a squeak from the door.

But as soon as he was out of the house, the old woman went quickly to the mouse-trap and set it off with the poker, so that it would do no harm to any mouse.

She made herself a cup of tea and sat down in her rocking chair by the fire.

"Are you there?" she called softly. "Are you there, window-elf and floor-elf and door-elf?"

She waited a moment but there was no answer, and she was afraid that the three elves had left her for ever. Then all at once a little gust of wind blew. She could tell there was a gust of wind, because it blew a puff of smoke down the chimney. And at the same time there was the sound of a little "rat-tattle, rat-tattle!" from the window. Full of happiness and excitement, for she knew the window-elf was back in his proper place, the old woman went quickly and tried the creaking board.

"Creak-creak, creak-creak!" went the board, just as before. Then the old woman went and tried the door.

"Squea-eak!" it said. "Squea-eak!" just as if it were saying "Thank you" to the old woman for letting the door-elf stay with her and not be sent away.

So that is how the three elves were allowed to stay in the old woman's cottage as her friends; and whenever she heard the door squeak or the floor creak or the window rattle, she thought how friendly her little noises were and she was glad to have them to keep her company.

And at night, before she fell asleep she would hear the little mouse patter-pattering on the floor, looking for any crumbs she had left him.

Eleven White Pigeons

I

KING REX reigned over a country whose name means 'The Kingdom of the Valleys'. His Queen was called by a name which means Pink Rhododendron Bud, but we will call her Queen Bud for short. "All my pink petals have fallen," she used to say, "and I am nothing but a withered stalk." Nevertheless, she was not unhappy. She had an eldest son called Sparrowhawk, four other sons and one daughter; she would sit for most of the day on a sofa in the royal apartments with her silk embroidery, a bottle of smelling-salts and the History of the Kingdom in thirty-six volumes, of which she had now read twelve.

As for the King, he was kind to her and treated her with great respect, listening to her opinion on all matters—all except those matters on which he was advised by the Lord Chancellor, a tall, thin man in black called Crabwitz. Chancellor Crabwitz was a most useful fellow, sticking seals and ribbons on all the papers which King Rex could not understand, and saving him endless trouble.

For the King did not like trouble. He was over fifty years old and thought it was time he had a quiet life. He had thought it was time he had a quiet life ever since he was about twenty-five, and so he had had. For his was a peaceful kingdom. Nobody worked hard. "Most people," he would say, "work themselves to death in order to become rich so that they can be lazy and not work any more. *My* people have more sense. They are lazy without going to the trouble of becoming rich first. So they enjoy life while they can. They go fishing, sing songs and listen to the band. Very sensible, I call it—don't you, Bud, my dear?"

"Well, perhaps you are right," said the Queen, "though what we should do if there were a war I can't imagine. We have no army, the people know nothing about fighting, and there are no stores and no guns in case of trouble."

"But why should there be trouble, my dear? Nobody ever makes war on us. What is there to make war about?"

"The people of the mountains made war upon us in the time of your ancestor Felix the Fortunate. I have been reading about it in Volume Ten of the History of the Kingdom."

"That was a long time ago," said the King comfortably. "They have learned sense since then."

"I hope so," said the Queen, "though in my opinion nobody ever learns sense."

"Well, my dear," said King Rex, "I have nothing

to fear as long as I have a sensible Queen like you and a sensible Chancellor like dear old Crabwitz. An excellent fellow, Crabwitz. He signs all my papers for me. He plays a very good game of chess too. Each time I play with him, I only *just* manage to beat him. That shows how good he is. There is only one thing I don't like about him—his bony legs. What a pity he has such very thin legs and such knobbly knees. They really look quite absurd in black stockings. Where do you think he gets black stockings narrow enough to fit such thin legs? I just can't imagine."

"As a matter of fact," said the Queen, "they are knitted for him by an old aunt who lives in a little room at the top of the west tower looking towards the mountains. She's quite mad, they say, and spends all her time knitting black stockings for her nephew and talking to her pigeons."

"Pigeons?" said the King. "Does she keep pigeons up there?"

"Oh yes," answered the Queen, "eleven white pigeons. She feeds them on crumbs and talks to them. You can see them fluttering round the windows at the top of the west tower on fine days."

The King looked out of the window.

"So you can," said he; for there, fluttering about in the sunlight, their white wings resting gracefully upon the air, were three or four white birds. How happy and carefree they looked, as they preened themselves on the grey stone sills of the windows at the top of the square tower.

"Now Rex, my dear," said Queen Bud in a voice which the King knew only too well, "don't forget what you have to do this morning."

"No, dear," said the King. "Will you stay and help me?"

"No," said the Queen. "I think you had better do it by yourself."

And taking up her silk embroidery, her smelling-salts and the History of the Kingdom, Volume Thirteen, she went off to her own apartments.

The King told a servant to call for the Princes and the Princess. Now the eldest Prince, Sparrowhawk, was a serious, hard-working young man of eighteen who was away at college in the neighbouring kingdom. He had been gone for nearly two years. But the other four Princes and the little Princess, whose ages were between sixteen and ten, were a merry, careless crew, who took nothing seriously and never seemed to want to do an hour's work. The Queen had made the King promise to give them a good talking-to. They were seldom all at home, but this morning a message had been sent to them and in a few minutes they all came trooping in, laughing and talking. They looked so full of fun that the King knew he was in for a difficult time. He managed to quieten them down, and then he spoke to the eldest. This was a boy of sixteen, whose name was Blackbird.

"Blackbird," said the King solemnly. "You are now sixteen. What have you learned to do?"

"Nothing, father," said Blackbird cheerfully.

"Nothing at all?" said the King unhappily. "What shall I tell your mother. She thinks—that is, she and I think—that every young man ought to have an occupation. Have you no occupation whatever."

"He can play the flute beautifully," said the second son.

"Really?" said the King. "I used to be able to do

that myself before I lost some of my front teeth."

"*You* played the flute, father?" said Blackbird, pulling a flute from the pocket of his jacket. "Let's hear you."

"No, no," said the King. "Not now. *You* play it. I'd rather like to hear how much you've learnt."

"Shall I?" asked Blackbird.

"Yes, do," said the others.

So Blackbird put the flute to his lips and blew a merry little tune which set the King's foot tapping on the royal footstool.

"Toot, toot, too——

Tuck-a tuck-a tuck-a tuck-a tuck-a TA!" said the flute.

"You see, father," explained the Princess, "when he was born, a blackbird used to come and sing on a tree just above his cradle. That is why he is called Blackbird, and that is why he can't help playing the flute."

"Well, he doesn't play it so badly," said the King. "Mind you, he hasn't quite got *my* touch, but he will learn. Now then," he went on, "who's next?"

The second son's name was Tortoiseshell, because when he was born a tortoiseshell cat used to walk about on the palace roof screeching and wailing in a most heart-breaking manner.

"What have you learnt to do in the course of your fourteen years?" asked the King.

"Nothing," said Tortoiseshell. "Nothing except playing the fiddle."

"You see, father," said the Princess, "how could he help learning to play the fiddle when he used to lie awake at night listening to that cat on the roof?"

"There's something in that," agreed the King. "Let's hear what you can do."

So Tortoiseshell put his fiddle to his chin, scraped a little to tune the strings, and played a tune.

"Dee, dee, dee——

Deedle, deedle, deedle, deedle, deedle, dee," said the fiddle.

"Not bad," said the King, "not bad at all. Mind you, I used to be able to play a bit before I got the rheumatism, and I could do a lot better than that. Still, he's young, and he may learn in time. Who's next?"

The next Prince was a boy called Bumble, because a big bumble-bee had buzzed all round his cradle when it was put in the palace gardens in the summer weather.

"What can *you* do?" asked the King. "Make honey?"

"No," said Bumble, "I can't even do that. I can't do anything."

"Except play the bass fiddle," said the Princess. "He plays it beautifully, father. You listen to him. He can give you a tickling feeling in the ears. Just listen."

So Bumble took his bass fiddle—what we should call a 'cello—which was standing beside the door, scraped a few notes to tune it, and began to play.

"Zoom, zoom-ba-zoom, zoom-ba-zoom——

Zoom-ba-zoom-ba-zoom-ba-zoom-ba-zoom!" said the bass-fiddle.

"Not bad at all," said the King.

"Did you feel a tickle inside your ears?" asked the Princess.

"Sort of," said the King. He had not felt it at all, but he was anxious to say the proper thing. "Of course when I was a young fellow, I too played the 'cello——"

Everybody laughed.

"That's a rhyme," cried the Princess. "You must be a poet, father. You can write us some words and we'll sing them."

"I don't think I could do that," said the King, "though when I was courting your mother, I turned out some very passable verses. However, we'd better get on. Who's next?"

The youngest son was a boy called Mountain Goat. When he was a baby, the Queen had not been very well so he was fed on milk from a goat that had been brought down specially from the hills. Now in that country a favourite instrument is the drum, and this is made, as everybody knows, by stretching a goat-skin tight across a wooden frame. So of course, when Mountain Goat grew up, he had learnt to play the drum.

"Let's hear you," said the King.

So Mountain Goat brought out his drum and beat it with two drumsticks.

"Br-r-room! br-r-room! br-r-room!

Boom, boom-ba-room, ta-TA! BOOM!" said the drum.

"Not bad at all," said the King. "I've heard worse. You might be quite good one day if you practise. And now what about you, my dear?" he asked of the Princess, who was by this time sitting on his knee. "You're only nine years old and I don't suppose you can do a thing. Can you?"

"I'm ten," said the Princess, "but you're quite right—I can do nothing, nothing at all."

"Oh yes, she can," said Mountain Goat. "When she was a baby, they put her cot outside in the fine sunny mornings and there was a tree just beside it with a few leaves left which used to twirl about in the breeze. That's why she's called Autumn Leaf, and that's why she dances all day."

"Oh, you dance, do you?" said the King. "Well, let's see what you can do!"

So the Princess slipped off the King's knee and did a few turns just to make her arms and legs loose.

"I'll tell you what we'll do," said the King. "We'll all play together and Autumn Leaf shall do a little dance. Then I shall be able to tell your mother you haven't altogether wasted your time."

He quickly went to his desk, and out of one of the drawers he took an instrument. It was an oboe. He put it to his lips and, to the astonishment of his children, played a merry little tune. He did it quite well, considering he was very out of practice.

"Wonderful!" they all cried. "Come on, let's start."

So the King and the four boys all began to play a gay dance tune, while the Princess twirled about on her toes, round and round, just like the autumn leaf she had been named after.

When everything was going well and getting really noisy, the Queen came in. So did Chancellor Crabwitz. His face was looking worried under his white wig and his thin legs were trembling with agitation. The music stopped and the Princess sank into a chair, quite out of breath with dancing.

There was a terrible silence. The Queen was sniffing powerfully at her smelling-salts. At last she spoke.

"Wouldn't you like *me* to *sing* to you?" she asked in a voice of frightful sarcasm.

"And perhaps *I* could join in with the bugle?" suggested Crabwitz.

"Oh, *could* you, Crabby?" asked the Princess.

"Be quiet," said the King. "He didn't mean it. He can play chess, but he can't play the bugle."

He looked at the Queen unhappily.

"I'm sorry, Bud," he said miserably. "You are quite right. We *were* making rather a noise. I wanted to prove to you that the children *can* do something after all. They haven't been wasting their time altogether, you see."

"Sit down," said the Queen, "and listen to me. If this is all you have learnt to do with your lives, you are an idle, good-for-nothing, ungrateful lot of children. It is most distressing. I imagined you would have learnt something serious; instead I find you fiddling and fluting as if you were the palace orchestra, which is paid to do all that. I don't know where we shall end, I really don't. You remind me of the family of your ancestor, King Rufus the Eighteenth; who joined a troupe of wandering actors and were all eaten by dragons. You can read the whole story in Volume Seven. I am utterly ashamed of you. I don't know what to say."

Here she began weeping and everyone looked very uncomfortable.

"But my dear," said King Rex tenderly, "there are no dragons nowadays. I really don't think things are as bad as you say——"

"Fortunately, your Majesty," said Crabwitz, "you have one son who has not wasted his time. The eldest Prince, Sparrowhawk, should be a great comfort to us all. A serious and devoted young man. I had news of him only this morning. His tutors at college speak most highly of him. He gained 97 marks out of 100 at the last examinations. A very distinguished performance."

This cheered everyone up, so that nothing more was said. The children went off to play with their friends, and the King settled down to a game of chess with the Chancellor, and the Queen sat on the sofa and calmed herself down with her silk embroidery.

2

A few months later, the King and Queen were having tea in the royal apartments. All at once there was a distant noise in the city, a noise of confused excitement. There had been a certain amount of commotion in the kingdom for some days, but the

King had taken little notice. He had mentioned it to Crabwitz, but Crabwitz had said there was nothing wrong, and that was good enough for the King.

Now, however, the noise became so loud that even the King could not ignore it. As it came nearer, he could make out the sound of shouting and marching, of a military band with drums and trumpets, and an occasional burst of cannon-fire. He went to the window and looked out. From where he stood, he could see the principal streets and squares of the city.

"Why, bless my soul!" he said to the Queen. "There are men in uniform marching, people shouting and waving banners, and no end of noise and excitement. What *can* be the matter?"

The Queen came and stood beside him. Even as he spoke, a column of soldiers marched into the square in front of the palace. There was a mob of people shouting and waving flags. "Long live the Kingdom of the Mountains, Long live the Kingdom of the Valleys! Down with King Rex! Long live Prince Sparrowhawk! Long live the Revolution!" These were some of the cries which the surprised King and Queen heard amidst the confusion.

"Dear me!" said the King. "Do you think the fire-brigade is having a practice, or——"

"Don't be stupid," said the Queen. "This is serious. It sounds like a Revolution to me."

"Impossible," said the King. "Why, we never have Revolutions in my country. Besides, Crabwitz would have told me about it. Where *is* Crabwitz, by the way? And where is the Palace guard?"

He rang the bell and sent servants running hither and thither, but the Chancellor was nowhere to be found. Nor was the palace guard, which was usually

cracking nuts and playing games in the courtyard
with the children of the royal servants. By this time
the mob was all round the palace and the soldiers
were at the gate. A very fierce-looking general with
an enormous black moustache hanging down over his
mouth was sitting on a black horse shouting orders.
He got off his horse and strode through the gates.

"I do believe he's coming in!" said the King
excitedly. "Do offer him some tea, my dear. I love
to see generals with big moustaches drinking tea."

"Don't be a fool!" said the Queen, who had turned
very pale.

Just then the tall double doors of the royal drawing-
room were thrown open and the fierce-looking
general stood before the King and Queen. Beside
him stood Crabwitz, the Chancellor, looking pale and
anxious. His stockings were wrinkled and his bony
knees knocked together. The general spoke. His
voice was deep and ferocious and his great black
moustache wobbled up and down vigorously as the
strange words poured forth.

"*Boggl tanto, boggl carpo!*" said the general. "*Het noo
marky marky het rumpf het bolgo! Twin iko bim hortico bim
crampstok tot fletso punny-unny het bolgopuliat in WALLOP!*"

"What does he say?" said the King, looking round
helplessly.

The Chancellor stepped forward.

"He bids your Majesty good afternoon——"

"Ask him if he'll have some tea."

Crabwitz ignored the interruption and went on.
"He is the general in charge of the army from the
Kingdom of the Mountains. He proclaims a Revolution in the name of your son, Sparrowhawk, and calls
upon you to give up your crown in favour of the

Prince, at whose request he has entered the country."

"Sparrowhawk?" asked the King in surprise. "My son a traitor? Impossible! Where is he?"

At this moment a tall, handsome, young man with dark, frowning brows stepped into the room.

"I am no traitor, Your Majesty," he said stiffly. "For some time I have been distressed at the way in which you have ruled the country. The people are idle and foolish. The country is poor, weak and defenceless. I have come to govern. I will make the Kingdom of the Valleys a great kingdom. I call upon you to give up your throne."

The Queen flung herself at his feet.

"My Son!" she cried. "Can this be true? Do you mean what you say? Is this what you have been learning at college?"

Sparrowhawk pushed his mother aside roughly.

"It is no use, Your Majesty," he said coldly. "My mind is made up. The people are with me. The Chancellor is with me. I have the army of the mountains to back me up. You have an hour to make up your mind. After that, I shall take over the throne by force. I call upon you to resign."

"Crabwitz," said the King pitifully. "How could you? Just when we were in the middle of a game of chess too. Who would have suspected *you*?"

"I am sorry, Your Majesty," said Crabwitz stiffly. "I had no choice. I did what I thought best."

He said something to the general.

"*Dohnanyi bartok*," answered the general, clicked his heels, saluted the King and Queen, and marched out. Crabwitz followed.

"Remember," said Sparrowhawk. "You have one hour."

He strode out after the others, leaving the unhappy King and Queen with two or three distracted servants.

There was a long and agitated discussion of what was to be done. The Queen wept and stormed, threatened vengeance, ran about the room and threw herself on the sofa. The King was very calm and cheerful.

"We must escape," he said. "We can't stay here."

The servants told him the palace was surrounded. What would become of the King and Queen if they resigned? What would become of them if they didn't? In the end it was decided that they should try to escape into the forest, where loyal subjects might look after them till the trouble was over. The royal laundry van stood at a side-entrance, ready loaded with the palace linen. With luck they could escape hidden inside it. There was not a minute to lose. A few bags were quickly packed, and the Queen insisted on taking with her the silk embroidery, her smelling-salts and the History of the Kingdom in thirty-six volumes, of which she had now read twenty-one. They decided to take with them one old and faithful servant called Peter, and his wife Griselda. There was no room for any more. Two hampers of food were packed. Then the four of them crept down a back stairway to the side entrance. The driver of the royal laundry van was a coachman whose parents had been in service with the King for fifty years. He said he would drive them wherever they wanted to go, as long as his horses could travel. It was late in the afternoon when the van passed unchallenged through the gates, between the avenues of trees in the royal park and out towards the open country. No one noticed anything out of the ordinary. The escape, so far, had been successful.

Presently, darkness began to fall. In a thick forest they decided to spend the night. Peter and Griselda prepared a meal, and afterwards they settled down to sleep.

"This is rather fun, you know," said the King to himself, but he said nothing to the Queen who was tired and unhappy.

They travelled on in this way for some days. The laundry van was not uncomfortable, and the two servants looked after the King and Queen as well as they were able. They saw very few people, for they were travelling through a lonely part of the kingdom. In a week's time they had eaten all the food in the hampers and had to buy more whenever they came to a village. They had forgotten to bring any money. The Queen had some jewellery with her, but it was difficult to sell jewels in country villages. Peter managed to sell some of the royal linen of which there were large quantities in the laundry van. However, it was not easy to sell linen sheets and pillow-cases that had not been washed. All the same, they managed to get enough to eat.

The days grew into weeks. They had little idea where they were going. Nor could they find out what was happening back in the city. No one seemed to have much news of the Revolution. Autumn was coming on fast, and the weather turned colder. Soon they were obliged to light fires in the woods to keep themselves warm. The Queen complained of the cold. The old servants began to be worried. They could not go on like this all the winter. They would have to find a hut or shelter somewhere and see if they could make themselves comfortable. The two horses travelled well, but they had not enough to eat and soon began to look thin. Each day the travellers hoped to find an empty hut or farm-building where they could hide, but they had no luck. They dared not tell anyone who they were in case there were enemies looking for them. At one place there was a small company of soldiers who asked awkward questions and wondered why the royal laundry van was travelling so far from the palace. This alarmed the Queen, and at the next village she made the coachman buy paint and brushes, and he and Peter set to work to paint over the royal coat of arms and the name of the laundry.

The weather grew terribly bad. It rained without stopping, and it was very cold besides. It was too wet for a fire to be lit. The King and Queen sat shivering inside the van.

"It's no good, Rex," the Queen said miserably. "We must make for a town, and there we must give ourselves up, tell them to take us back home, and throw ourselves on our son's mercy."

"Oh, I wouldn't like to do that," said the King. "We might be put in those awful damp dungeons with chains on our feet."

"We might just as well be in a dungeon as here," said the Queen.

"Well," said the King. "Let us give ourselves another day. If we don't find a hut to-morrow, or a friendly peasant who will take us in for the winter, we will do as you say."

But he had little hope. The countryside was becoming mountainous and even more deserted. Rain was falling. Night was coming on. They were entering a thick wood. The road began to rise steeply uphill, and the poor horses were panting and straining.

Suddenly they stopped and pricked up their ears.

A most unusual sound could be heard faintly, through the noise of the rain on the leaves. It was the sound of music—music and voices. This was such an unexpected sound that all five travellers, and the two horses as well, stopped to listen.

"People," said the King. "Undoubtedly people. What can they be doing shouting and singing in such a place as this?"

"What shall we do?" the two servants asked.

"Go straight on," said the King. "If they are friends we are saved; if they are enemies, at least we shall find out what is going to happen to us."

The coachman shouted to the horses, which heaved and strained, and presently the van was lumbering up the hill once more. And there, for the time being, let us leave them.

3

What had been happening all this time in the rest of the kingdom, and what had been happening to the five other children of the King and Queen?

Well, soon after their talk with the King, the Princes Blackbird, Tortoiseshell, Bumble and Mountain Goat, and the Princess Autumn Leaf, had formed themselves into a troupe of travelling musicians and began to play at fairs and markets in the nearby towns. In this way they had earned enough money to keep themselves. The summer was fine and they lived in the open. They had never enjoyed anything so much in their lives. They played merrily, and little Autumn Leaf was a delightful dancer, so that soon they began to be quite well known in the small towns and the villages. There were other troupes of musicians and actors as well, for the country was very fond of amusements and dancing. Of course you may say it was a scandalous and surprising thing for the royal family to be going on in this way, but nobody was much concerned as to who they were. It is true that Crabwitz and other royal advisers occasionally told the King that something ought to be done about it, but somehow nothing ever was.

"Leave them alone," said the King, "and they'll come home as soon as the weather begins to turn cold."

Then the Revolution happened. The army from the Kingdom of the Mountains marched in, the King and Queen fled, and Sparrowhawk was proclaimed King. At first it made little difference to people's everyday lives. The new King was busy arranging Committees of this and that. Then the Committees began to get moving. Sparrowhawk and his advisers had decided that the people were lazy and thoughtless, spending their time amusing themselves instead of working. So they made some very strict laws. One of these said that all music and dancing were to stop, except for a few special bands which only played in the big towns on public holidays.

All musicians were ordered to give up their instruments and get work on the farms or in newly organised workshops. Soldiers were sent round to see that they obeyed.

The four Princes and the Princess did not like the sound of this at all. They had made a good deal of money by the end of the summer, and with this they bought a caravan, a horse, a cooking-stove, and a great deal of food and warm clothing. They set off towards the wild regions near the border where they hoped to be left alone. As they went through the villages, they gave concerts and played at dances, so that they earned still more money to keep themselves through the winter. These dances were, of course, forbidden by law; but in the smaller and more distant villages little notice was as yet taken of the new law, and there were few soldiers to enforce it.

As they went they were joined by other musicians and by actors and dancers, jugglers, singers and all sorts of people who were off to escape from the new laws.

By the time autumn came, they had found themselves three warm, dry caves in the hills, far away from the big cities; here they all made themselves into a colony, working by day to make the things they would need, and singing and dancing and playing their instruments in the evening. When they felt it was time they had more money or wished to buy blankets or food, they sent out parties into the towns and villages.

The whole band—nearly a hundred of them altogether—were perfectly happy, and worried very little about what would happen to them in the end. They made Blackbird into a kind of Chief or General, because he was fair and everybody liked him. Besides, he was the eldest of the Princes, so it seemed right that he should have the leading position.

One wet evening in late autumn, soon after they had lit a huge fire in the biggest of the caves and started their singing and dancing, two men, who were returning late from an expedition, reported to Blackbird that they had seen a strange thing.

"A huge van," they said, "drawn by two tired horses, is coming up the hill. We did not stop to find out what it was, but came straight to tell you."

A party was sent out to see what this strange thing could be. They very soon came back to report.

"A laundry van," said the leader of the party, "containing a hundred and forty-seven sheets, two hundred and three pillow-cases, ninety-six towels and the King and Queen!"

And at that moment the van struggled up the track and stopped at the entrance to the cave.

"Father!" shouted Blackbird, just like a schoolboy, quite forgetting that he was the general of an outlaw colony.

"Mother!" cried the other Princes and the little Princess.

The King and Queen, helped by Peter and Griselda, got down from the van, the coachman followed with their luggage, the horses were taken off and fed and rubbed down, and a wonderful meal was prepared by the cooks on duty for the day.

There is no need to describe that meal. No doubt it was not as good as the royal feasts of the old days, but it was better than anything the King and Queen had tasted for months. The Queen wept for joy; so busy was she embracing the Princes and hugging her only daughter that she could hardly eat. As for the King, he was too busy eating to embrace anyone until there was no more food. Afterwards he made up for it.

After supper they settled down to talk. The King told how he had been forced to resign by the wicked eldest Prince and the treacherous Crabwitz, and the Princes told what little news they had heard about the state of the kingdom after they had taken to their caravan and fled.

"I never did like that Crabwitz," said the Princess. "He was always telling me to go and brush my hair."

"Yes," said Tortoiseshell, "and do you know what we heard in one of the villages? They said that his aunt, who everyone thought was mad, was really a spy. She lived up in the tower in our very own palace and sent out her pigeons with messages to Sparrow-hawk and his friends in the Mountain Kingdom!"

"Well, fancy that," said the King, astonished. "The eleven white pigeons. So they carried messages, did they—and the old aunt wasn't mad at all. I might have known that a woman who knitted stockings like those wasn't to be trusted!"

The leader of the orchestra came up and bowed respectfully to the King and Queen and offered to play to them.

The King thanked him graciously, and the leader collected his players together. They performed some lively music, to which the Princess and several other children danced.

66

"Very enjoyable," said the King, turning to the Queen. "Really, my dear, you must admit that the children have made most remarkable progress. I'm quite proud of them. And of all the children, it seems to me that our own little Autumn Leaf dances with the most lightness and charm."

Queen Bud smiled. For the first time for weeks, she was quite happy.

"Yes," she said, "if they had to waste their time, this is as good a way as any. And I must own," she added, "that Sparrowhawk has turned out to be rather a disappointment."

Of course the King and Queen were invited to stay with the outlaw band, and they contributed greatly to everyone's comfort by making them a present of the royal sheets and pillow-cases, of which a specially appointed washing party took charge the following day. It was a little difficult to dry them in the rainy weather, but in time they were quite dry and even ironed.

The time passed happily enough. There were one or two alarms, but it was not difficult to hide the King and Queen if any danger threatened. Soon the winter came on, and the whole encampment was snow-bound, so that they were safer than ever. The King had brought his oboe with him and was able to take an honoured place in the orchestra, though it was not always easy for the conductor to bring himself to tell His Majesty when he was not playing in tune. As for the Queen, she had long since used up all her silk and finished all thirty-six volumes of the History of the Kingdom, so that she developed quite a keen interest in music. As a girl she had danced gracefully, and she was able to teach the children some new steps.

Then in the spring came the news that everyone was waiting for. It was a bright sunny day. A party had gone to the village for food, and when they returned they told how everyone was running about excitedly and telling each other the great news which had come from the city. The Revolution, it seemed, was over. Everywhere people were asking for King Rex back again. Bells were being rung, schools were closed, flags were hung from the windows, and there was singing and shouting.

What had happened was this. The army of the Mountain Kingdom, under the ferocious general with the black moustache, was very large and was becoming a nuisance. It ate up all the food, slept in all the best beds, tramped all over the place talking its strange language, and generally became most unpopular.

King Sparrowhawk summoned the general and told

him that, since the Revolution had succeeded and everything was orderly and peaceful, he must take his men away.

"*Sobranie poosgka*," said the general. "*Marky marky, het bojum, kodaly wopska!*"

This meant that his army were enjoying themselves and did not want to go home at all. After that there were dreadful disturbances everywhere. People refused to give the soldiers food and the soldiers themselves became discontented and thought they might as well go home and see what their families were up to. Meanwhile, Sparrowhawk had been drilling an army from among his own people, and he threatened to go to war with the mountain people and turn them out. So in the end the mountain people were forced to go home, and the valley people's army was in charge of the country. Now nobody enjoyed these goings-on, because the valley people were most peaceful; moreover, they hated the new laws about working hard and not playing music or going to plays or having dances. So there was a new Revolution led by the important people in the army. They marched into the palace and took charge of Sparrowhawk and Crabwitz and even Crabwitz's old aunt, whose pigeons were considered to have caused a great deal of trouble. It was decided to ask the old King, Rex, and Queen Bud to take the throne once more—that is, if only they could be found. But nobody in the city knew where they were. Search-parties were sent out in all directions, and a valuable reward was offered to the person who should bring the first definite news of Their Majesties. Proclamations were proclaimed, and heralds with trumpets went on swift horses to all the villages and cities.

Of course it was not long before the King and Queen were found. The outlaws in the cave, as soon as they knew for certain that the Revolution was over, told the people in the village, and the people in the village told those in the town. Messengers came from the army, who were in charge in the city, and a body-guard came to take the King and Queen back in triumph. A splendid red coach was sent, but the King and Queen said they would like to go back in the laundry van, which had been their only home for so long. Peter and Griselda went with them. They had fresh horses, but these were driven by the same coachman who had taken them away on the day of the Revolution. Behind them came the four Princes and the Princess in their caravan, and then followed the rest of the outlaws. Then came a host of villagers and townspeople in carts or on horseback. As you can imagine, they moved slowly. But how joyful everyone was! There was singing and shouting and waving of flags. The weather was fine, the birds sang gaily in the freshly budding trees, and wherever they went the children danced in the streets and the dogs barked with excitement.

There is not much more to tell. At last the procession reached the city, and the King and Queen and their children were back in the royal palace. With new advisers the King set to work—quite energetically for him—to put everything right again. The hard laws were done away with. All the same, people had got into the habit of doing a certain amount of work, and they did not go back to their lazy ways altogether.

There was the question of what to do with Sparrow-hawk, Crabwitz and his old aunt. They had been thrown into the palace dungeons, where they lived miserably and uncomfortably for a fortnight. The dungeons were dark and damp, and full of toadstools, spiders and other annoyances.

"Put them to death!" said the fiercest of the King's advisers.

"Send them out of the country!" said another.

"Leave them in the dungeon!" said a third.

But the four Princes and the Princess pleaded with their father to be kind to them. They did not have to plead long, because the King was a kind man.

"I'll tell you what," said Mountain Goat. "There's going to be a public holiday and celebration next Monday. Let the three of them out of prison and make them dance in the main square. Everybody will enjoy it, and it won't do them any harm."

"Good idea!" said Bumble. "It'll teach them not to try any more Revolutions and spoil people's fun."

"A very good idea," agreed the King, and all the advisers, including the Queen, were of the same opinion. So it was announced that on the Monday there would be dancing in the main square, to be led by Sparrowhawk, Crabwitz and the old aunt, who would perform on a special platform to the accompaniment of the outlaws' orchestra.

That scene must be left to the imagination. As you may suppose, the old Chancellor with his thin legs was no dancer; nor was his aunt; as for Sparrowhawk, dancing was not one of the things he had learnt at college. So the three of them were a very funny sight indeed. They caused much merriment and did not enjoy themselves; but everyone agreed that such a punishment was much less than they deserved for having caused so much trouble.

Crabwitz was allowed to go and live in a cottage in

the country with his aunt, where she was obliged to knit woollen stockings for the children of the palace servants; but she was never again allowed to keep pigeons. One other change was made after the return of the King and Queen. It was decided to keep up a small army in case there was ever trouble again; Sparrowhawk was put in charge of it, and a very capable and hard-working general he made.

Now we must finish the story by saying, as everyone else did before they went to bed on that famous public holiday, "Long Live King Rex and Queen Bud." A long time they did live, too, and the whole of their exciting and prosperous reign is well described—far better than I could describe it—in the History of the Kingdom of the Valleys, Volume Thirty-Seven.

Little Monday

THERE was once a baker, who lived with his wife and their two children in a house on the edge of a town. He baked all the bread for the people in that part of the town, and twice a week he made cakes. His wife cooked and sewed and washed for her family, and on market-days she went into town to buy everything that was needed for the household.

They had two children and no more. Tom was about eleven years old and his sister was eight. Although she was only eight, Frances was fond of sewing and had already become quite clever. She would mend for her mother or make simple things such as dusters. Best of all she liked to make clothes for her dolls out of pieces of bright curtain material which her mother did not want. Tom helped his father in the bakery, which was warm and dark and smelt of bread; or else he did odd jobs in the garden or about the house, and in the evenings he would sit at a corner of the big table in the living-room and do his lessons.

Tom and Frances did not play much with other children—not because they did not like them, but because there were not many children of their age in that part of the town. Besides, they were very fond of each other and would play happily together for hours.

Tom would mend his sister's dolls if their arms and legs came loose, as they sometimes did; and Frances would help Tom with his toy soldiers and his trains. In the fine weather they would go off together to the fields outside the town.

As for the baker, he was a very busy man who did not say much and was nearly always covered with flour and smelt of warm, crisp, new bread. When his work was done, he would come in and sit in a high, hard chair and put on his steel spectacles and read the newspaper or the Bible or some other book.

It was rather a serious family, you might say, but all four of them were happy. None of them seemed to want the bright lights of the town in the evening, or smart clothes, or money to jingle in their pockets. They were not rich, but they did not spend very much, and the baker saved a good deal of what he earned.

The house was small but comfortable, and the baker's wife kept it clean and tidy. Sometimes, but not very often, they had friends in to tea on Sunday; and sometimes the baker's wife would have a chat with her neighbour over the garden wall. Occasionally the baker would go to the public house along the road for a drink and a smoke and to talk about the weather or the state of the country with his fellow-tradesmen.

One very wet evening in the late autumn the baker's family were all sitting round the fire in the living-room. The tea-things had been cleared away and washed up, and the table had been pulled near the fire. It was cold as well as wet. The big oil-lamp stood in the middle of the table, casting its glow on Tom's school books and on his mother's pile of mending. Frances was making a nightdress for one of her dolls out of a piece of an old sheet. The baker was sitting in his high-backed chair reading the news-paper.

"A terrible evening," the baker's wife said for the third or fourth time. "I don't remember such an evening for goodness knows how long."

Nobody said anything. Indeed it was difficult to talk because of the noise of the rain on the roof and the gusty wind howling in the chimney and rattling the window-frames.

A few minutes later the baker took his pipe from his mouth and said:

"Do you think you could fasten that window a little tighter, Tom, my boy? There's a draught a-blowing down my neck."

Tom did as he was told. Again the wind howled, and now the window did not rattle so much. But there was soon a rattling at the door instead.

"Dear me, dear me," said the baker. "It's a terrible bad wind. I don't remember such a wind for goodness knows how long. I shall have to go and shut down my bakehouse oven or 'twill be out before morning."

He knocked his pipe out on the hearth, put down his newspaper and got up. There was another gust of wind and even more rain on the roof. Then the door rattled again. Everyone sat up and listened, for a voice was distinctly heard saying:

"Let me in! Oh please let me in!"

The baker went to the door and opened it.

On the doorstep was a very small girl with only a thin dress to cover her, a pair of ragged black stockings and worn-out shoes, and no hat or coat. The rain was pouring from her clothes and from her tangled black hair, which hung in streaks down her pale, wet face. She was shivering with cold and every inch of

75

her thin body seemed to be rattling with fear and streaming with water.

"Come in, child," said the baker. "Come in and let's get the door a-closed before we be all blown away."

He pulled the little girl across the threshold, where she stood dripping on the doormat while they all looked at her.

"Come away and get beside the fire," said the baker's wife. She put down her mending and led the child to the fire. Puddles began to form on the hearth-rug.

"Best get her dry," said the baker, "then we can give her something to eat; then maybe she won't catch her death of cold."

The baker's wife took her into the kitchen, dried her and gave her some warm clothes of Frances' instead of her own sopping rags. These were put straight into the sink to be washed. Then the little girl was given a seat at the table nearest the fire, and the baker brought her a piece of meat pie and some bread and butter and a mug of hot milk with sugar in it. The little girl ate hungrily and all the time she said nothing.

"Now then," said the baker, when she had nearly finished her meal, "let's have a little talk. For I suppose you *can* talk, my dear?"

"Oh yes," said the little girl brightly. "I can talk plenty when I want to."

Then she added, "But I don't want to sometimes."

And she laughed in a queer sort of way without smiling.

She was a funny looking urchin, the baker's wife was thinking. How very plain she was with her little close-set eyes and dark straight hair and wide mouth showing most of her teeth.

"Well, perhaps you'll tell us what your name is?" went on the baker.

"Monday," said the little girl.

"I know 'tis Monday," said the baker. "I know 'tis Monday, 'cos 'twas Sunday yesterday, but I asked you your name."

Again the little girl laughed without smiling.

"That *is* my name," she said. "I'm called Monday because it was on a Monday I was born. My mother told me."

"What a funny name," said Frances. Then she thought this might sound rude, so she said: "I mean, what a *queer* name. I've never heard it before. How old are you?"

"Nine or ten," said Monday. "Ten or nine—I can't remember which."

She did not look nine or ten, because she was so

77

very small—smaller than Frances in fact. But she might have been just nine, thought the baker's wife.

"Where's your mother now, little Monday?" said the baker. "You must tell us where she lives, for we'll have to be taking you back there when this rain stops."

"I haven't a mother," said the little girl. "No, nor a father; and I don't live *any*where. You'll just have to keep me, I'm afraid."

This surprised everyone. They all stopped for a minute and thought.

"If you haven't got a mother," said Tom, "how could she tell you when you were born. You said you knew you were born on a Monday because your mother said so."

"That's right," said the baker's wife, proud of her son's cleverness.

"Oh, that was a long time ago," said Monday. "I haven't got a mother *now*. That's what I meant."

It seemed there was nothing to be done that night except to keep little Monday and put her to bed. Then in the morning the baker could go to the police and find out what was to be done with her. So she was put to bed with Frances, who was very interested in her new companion but was not quite sure whether she liked her.

In the morning the baker remembered that owing to the arrival of little Monday he had forgotten to attend to the oven the night before. In the strong wind it had burnt out. Instead of going to the town to see the police, he had to light the stove again, and this made him late with his baking. His wife had to dry and clean the mats on which Monday had stood when she was dripping with rain the night before. Tom said at breakfast:

"She's a funny little thing, isn't she? Don't know that we want her living here."

But Frances was not quite so sure.

"Perhaps she'll play with me when I get in from school before you."

Then Monday came in for her breakfast, and they stopped talking.

2

Before tea-time, the baker had been into town and his wife had had several talks with the neighbours. But nobody had the least idea whom little Monday belonged to or where she came from. Monday herself did not seem to know either. She had been living, she said, with some other people in a house a long way away, and last night they had said very unkind things to her about the trouble she was causing them, so she had slipped out when they were not looking and walked into town through the rain.

"Perhaps these other people will put up a notice saying you are lost," said the baker's wife, "or perhaps they'll come looking for you themselves."

"I don't think so," said Monday. "They didn't like me much."

So it was decided that Monday should stay with the baker's family for the time being, as long as she promised not to make too much trouble and to help all she could.

After tea she agreed to help dry up the tea-things. Except for breaking a cup and a saucer, she did this very well and quite willingly. Then she offered to help Frances make her doll's nightdress.

"Can you sew?" asked Frances.

"Oh yes," said Monday, "give it to me. I'll show you."

She took the sewing and sat by the fire and got on with it while Frances undressed her dolls for bed. But when Monday finished sewing, it was found that she had stitched up the ends of the sleeves so that the dolls could not get their arms through. The night-dress looked so funny that everyone laughed. The baker's wife had to unpick the stitches and finish the work herself. Monday laughed too in that queer way of hers, and Frances, though she had laughed, was not at all sure that she was pleased.

Next day the baker's wife went to see Frances' teacher, and it was agreed that Monday should go to school. But Monday refused to go. Nothing would make her. The baker's wife took her along to the school, and no sooner had she returned home than little Monday followed her into the house.

"That's a silly place," said Monday. "I couldn't possibly stay there."

Try as she would, the baker's wife could not make Monday stay at school, so in the end she allowed her to spend her time at home, running round and doing odd jobs, playing in the garden and chasing stray cats. She went into the bakehouse with the baker, but she burnt her fingers and got in the way, and in the end he had to forbid her to go there again.

One evening Tom left his lesson books open on the table with a bottle of ink and a pen beside them. Frances was helping her mother in the kitchen and the baker was in the bakehouse mixing the cakes for the following day. When Tom came back, he found that Monday had been helping him with his lessons and had accidentally spilt ink all over his clean page. He was very angry, very angry indeed.

"What did you go and do that for?" he said. "Now I shall have to tear out the page and start all over again."

"I was only trying to help. Don't be cross with me, Tom, *please*," she begged.

All the same Tom was angry.

"You needn't do it again now," said Monday. "It's Saturday tomorrow, so you can play. Come on, let's get the trains out. We can have a wonderful game while Francie's in the kitchen."

So they got the trains out, and Monday had all sorts of ideas for new and interesting games with them. Soon Frances came in from the kitchen.

"Oh, you might have waited for me," she said. "You know I love playing with the trains."

"Well you can play now," said Tom. "Come on, let's put the rails together again and get out the goods vans."

But now Monday no longer wanted to play; she sat in a corner and made nasty remarks.

When the baker came in from his work, she went up to him and said:

"You'll be terribly cross with me, I'm afraid."

"Oh dear," said the baker, "and why should I be cross with you, eh?"

He sat down by the fireplace. Monday did not answer his question but got up on his knee and said:

"I'm sorry you're going to be cross with me because then you won't want to sing to us."

"Oh, I'm a-going to sing to you, am I?" asked the baker. "What makes you think I can sing, eh?"

"Oh, but you can," said Monday. "I've heard you

singing to yourself in the bakehouse when you thought nobody was listening."

"And what were you a-doing in the bakehouse?" asked the baker. "I thought I told you you weren't never to go there any more."

"I didn't think you meant it," said Monday, grinning and showing all her teeth. "Besides, how could I sweep up the floor if I didn't go in?"

"So it's you who's been a-sweeping up my floor," said the baker. "Well, may I ask you, did you see my pipe by any chance, for I think it fell out of my pocket when I was a-stooping down by the oven."

"Yes," said Monday, "I did see your pipe, and I swept it up and threw it into the fire. I tried to get it out but I was too late, and I saw it burning there along with the other rubbish."

"Well, you're the stupidest, wastefullest little urchin I've ever seen," said the baker, getting angry. "What did you want to come a-interfering in my bakehouse at all for, after I'd told ye not to, I should like to know?

"I'm terribly sorry," said Monday, the tears beginning to show in her little black eyes. "I'm terribly sorry, truly I am. Anyway," she went on, as the baker's wife came in from the kitchen, "you shouldn't smoke that nasty dirty pipe. Mother says so; I've heard her say so lots of times."

"Did you say that?" said the baker angrily, turning to his wife.

"Maybe I did, maybe I didn't," said the baker's wife. "What's it to do with *her* whether I said it or not?"

By this time Frances and Tom were quarrelling about what to play, because Frances wanted to play with the trains, while Tom was tired of them.

"No," said Tom. "I'm going to put them away, and then I'm going to read."

"I'll help you, Tom," said Monday.

"No," said Frances, "I'll help. Let me, Tom, please."

"I helped get them out," said Monday.

"I want to help put them away," said Frances.

"You shan't," said Monday, "I want to."

Then Frances began to cry.

"There you are," said the baker's wife, now thoroughly annoyed with her husband and her children. "Now look what you've done. You've made Francie cry. Never mind what the horrid little girl says, my duck. You shall help Tom put the trains away, so you shall."

Monday was by now sitting in the middle of the floor trying to fit an engine and a railway-signal into a cardboard box. She began to laugh.

"As for you," went on the baker's wife, turning to Monday, "you're a troublemaker, that's what you are—nothing but a nasty, low-down, mean, sneaking, impudent little troublemaker!"

Monday laughed still louder. How she was enjoying herself!"

"I love trouble," said little Monday between her laughs. "Oh I love it, I love it, I *love* it!"

"Be quiet, you nasty little too-clever-by-half——"

"I do so love trouble! Don't you, Tom? I can't help it, I'm made that way."

So Monday went on laughing, and the baker's wife scolded, Frances cried, the baker tried to find himself another pipe, and Tom went on putting the trains away; and this wasn't easy because little Monday was rolling about in the middle of the room and getting in the way.

Presently the noise died down and everyone felt rather unhappy. Monday got up from the floor and went across to the baker and put her elbows on his knees and looked up at him with her ugly little face.

"Now what about that song?" she asked. "You were going to sing to us. Oh, please sing to us."

"Oh yes, Dad, *do*!" said Frances, wiping away her tears.

The baker didn't want to sing to them, but it seemed the best thing to do. So he sat Frances on one knee and Monday on the other and put his arms round their middles.

"I don't know any smart songs," he said. "I can't remember the words; but such scraps as I know I'll sing to you gladly, if it'll keep you quiet and stop you for ever fuming and mischief-making."

And in a rather rusty voice the baker began to sing.

"Now comes the spring with flowers so bright,
    The birds have long been woken.
The Christmas tree has withered away,
    And Christmas toys are broken.
        Fala, fala!
Now is this not the silliest song,
    That ever was sung or spoken?"

The baker stopped for a moment to think.

"What a silly song!" said Monday.

"Never mind," said Tom, who had now packed up his trains and drawn near to listen. "Go on, Dad."

The baker cleared his throat and went on.

"I gave to my true love a cup,
    'Twas but a foolish token,
  But long before the month was up,
    The loving cup was broken.
        Fala, fala!
  But long before the month was up,
    The loving cup was broken."

"What do you want to sing that stuff for?" said the baker's wife. " 'Taint sense."

"I can't understand it," said Frances, "but it's nice. Isn't there any more?"

"It *is* silly," said Monday, "but you sing it nicely, so do go on."

"There's a lot more of it," said the baker, "but I can't think of the words. So now, my dears, if you want any more, you must sing for yourselves."

So they all sang the songs they had learnt at school, and the evening, which had started with quarrelling, ended happily for everyone.

3

After that, Monday did not cause quite so much trouble for a time. She still refused to go to school. Nor did the baker's wife want to let her help in the house, because she broke things and got in the way. One day she was followed into the house by a little scraggy grey cat with only one ear. The cat would not leave her, so it had to be adopted. It was a good mouser, but it was not a very clean cat as most cats are, and the baker's wife did not like it. All the same, the children were fond of it, for it would rub itself against their legs and tickle them. It sometimes scratched, and then the baker's wife would get angry and try to throw it out. But either the children stuck up for it, or else it was put out of the door and returned again as soon as possible, so that the baker's wife gave up trying to get rid of it.

Little Monday did not stay good for very long. If the baker's wife put clean clothes on her, they were sure to be torn and dirty before the day was out. If the baker left his spectacles and his books on a shelf beside the fire, Monday upset them for him and lost his place. Tom's toys would be left out in the rain and Frances' dolls soon began to look as untidy and dirty as Monday herself. She was a hopeless child, perfectly hopeless. It seemed as if nothing could be done about her. Yet she was never really sorry. She simply enjoyed being a nuisance. She laughed as if all her teeth would fly out when her grey cat tangled up the baker's wife's knitting when she was in the middle of making a winter vest for the baby that had been born next door.

The baker's wife talked a lot more over the garden wall than she had used to, and now it was always about little Monday that she talked. She told the neighbours what a terrible trial the child was and what a lot of bother she caused. The neighbours asked why she didn't try to send Monday to a home for naughty children, but the baker's wife said she didn't quite feel like doing that, and besides, she did not know how to set about it. So things went on as before. It seemed as if little Monday had come to stay for ever, and as if she would never get any better and always be a terrible trial and a bother.

One evening things were worse than usual. The whole family had been annoyed by little Monday. She was now sitting in the middle of the floor stroking her ugly grey cat. Tom was doing his lessons, Frances was reading a book, the baker's wife was polishing a pair of candlesticks, and the baker was trying to mend the side of his glasses which Monday had broken.

"She's a dratted nuisance," he said. "How can I read my newspaper with my specs all a-broken; that's what I'm asking?"

"It's no great matter for that," said his wife. "There's never anything in the paper—I've often heard you say so. But where am I going to find breakfast for us all when she's broken every egg that I bought from the grocer only yesterday?"

"And why did she go and leave my new pram out in the garden, so that the rain has spoilt it?" said poor Frances.

"And why do you go messing about with my books when I'm not looking and leaving dirty marks on the pages?" asked Tom.

But little Monday said nothing, and only sat and fondled her one-eared cat. All the same, she was not laughing. She was looking thoughtful and rather sad.

"What have we all done to be troubled so by a worthless, good-for-naught, bothersome urchin that is no good to nobody?" said the baker. "It's not as if we were evil folk like the Philistines or Pharaoh of Egypt, to be troubled with all the twelve plagues rolled into one. We're good folk we are—hard-working and as honest as most. What have we done to deserve *you*, I should like to know?"

But little Monday looked at him thoughtfully, and all she said was:

"There's no sense in plaguing *wicked* people. They make enough trouble for themselves."

"Why plague *anybody*?" asked the baker's wife crossly. "Isn't there trouble enough in the world without making more?"

Monday sighed.

"I can't help it," she said. "I just can't help it. Besides I do love it so."

Everybody made angry noises and went out of the room—everyone except Frances, who went on reading her book.

Monday went across to Frances and put her arms round her and began crying.

"You don't like me, Francie, do you? You all hate me."

"We like you all right really," said Frances. "Only why do you do such naughty things? You needn't have left my pram out in the garden. And why did you go and put mud on my lovely new pinafore?"

"I couldn't help it," said Monday. "Pinafores are such silly things. It looked so funny on you—all clean and white and covered with silly lambs and things."

"Lambs *aren't* silly," said Frances.

"Anyway, if you loved me, you wouldn't mind a bit of mud on your pinny. Your mother can wash it off. She likes washing."

"She doesn't," said Frances.

"Well, why does she do so much of it then? You hate me, all of you. That's all about it."

And once more she began to cry. Frances saw that it was no use arguing with her, so she went on reading her book.

After tea little Monday was nowhere to be found. Nor was the grey cat to be seen. Nobody bothered. They were probably out together doing mischief somewhere, and it was a relief not to have them in the house. They all settled peacefully down to their tasks till it was nearly time for bed. Everyone pretended not to care where Monday was, but privately they were all a little worried. The weather outside was rather horrid. It was not exactly raining, but there was a damp gusty wind, and the baker said he thought it would be a stormy night.

Then suddenly he sniffed and got up from his chair.

"What's that smell?" he said.

They all sniffed.

"Smells like burning to me," said the baker's wife. "Now what did I leave in the oven?"

But the smell was not coming from the oven, it was coming from outside.

The baker went towards the outer door, but it was flung open in his face, and the untidy figure of little

Monday appeared on the threshold in a gust of showery wind.

"Better look out!" she cried. "The bakehouse is burning!"

"You young demon!" shouted the baker. "What have you been up to now?"

Monday did indeed look like a demon. Her hair was partly burnt away and her face was blackened and bleeding. Her clothes were torn. A sleeve had been ripped quite away and one of her stockings was down to her ankle. Water dripped from what was left of her clothes.

She began to laugh. The baker made a grab for her, but she rushed out into the yard towards the burning bakehouse. The baker followed her. His wife and the children quickly put coats on and went after him.

The flames were rushing upwards and great clouds

of black smoke were blown here, there and everywhere
by the wind. There was not enough rain to quench
the fire. There was a crackling of burning timber.
Little Monday was running to and fro, staggering
under the weight of a bucket of water, constantly
refilled from a barrel in the yard, which she threw on
to the flames. The baker and the others ran for more
buckets; and, choked with smoke, they poured them
upon the fire from as near as they could approach.
Presently some neighbours came and lent a hand, and
someone ran for the fire brigade. But it was hopeless.
The fire became fiercer and fiercer. Soon they could
not get near enough to reach the flames with buckets
of water. They had to stand back and watch the bakehouse burn. Frances was crying beside her mother.
Suddenly Tom said:

"Where's Monday?"

The little girl was found lying on the ground near
the empty water barrel, choking and gasping with
smoke and exhaustion. The baker carried her indoors,
took her upstairs, and laid her on the bed.

"What did you do it for?" said the baker sadly.
"Whatever did you set my bakehouse afire for?"

He gave her some water, and she tried to sit up but
sank back again. Then she said feebly:

"I didn't, truly I didn't. It wasn't me, I tell you."

Then she fainted, and the baker's wife covered her
with the bedclothes to keep her warm, first taking off
her wet things. The others came upstairs and stood
beside the bed.

In the morning the bakehouse was found to be quite
burnt down. It was still smoking and smouldering,
but little of it was left standing. The fire brigade had
come too late.

Monday was better, but still very feeble. Between gasps and coughs she told them what had happened. She had been for a walk, and as she came back towards evening she had heard two men talking. She had hidden and listened. At first she could not hear what they said. Then she heard that they were going to set something on fire. How surprised she was when she heard that it was nothing else than the baker's bakehouse. They muttered something about the price of bread, and how it was too high, and people couldn't pay so much for their bread. This would teach them, they said. This would make them think. Monday did not understand all this, but she knew there was going to be trouble, and she liked trouble. Where there was trouble, there would she be. She followed the men carefully so as not to be seen. She thought of running on and telling the baker, but she did not see how she could pass them without being seen. They sneaked into the bakehouse, and Monday went in after them. One of them was carrying a tin of something. He splashed it about, spreading it as fast as he could over the floor and walls. He emptied the last of it on to a pile of old flour sacks. Then the other one said, "That'll do," and took out a box of matches. He struck one of them and threw it into the flour sacks. Then, when the sacks began to flare up, the first man said, "Come on!" and both of them ran out of the building. That was the last Monday saw of them. She had been hiding behind the oven so that they should not see her. The flour sacks were behind the door, and Monday only got out with the greatest difficulty. She was not at all frightened because she enjoyed trouble. She knew just what to do. Seizing the pail that always stood beside the water barrel in a corner of the yard, she filled it and ran back into the bakehouse. She threw it on the flames and went for more. She did this several times, until she began to feel tired. The fire kept breaking out in different places. When she knew she couldn't put it out she had gone to the house and told the baker.

When her story was finished, Monday lay back on the bed and closed her eyes. Nobody said anything.

"What a story!" thought the baker's wife to herself. "Wonder where those two men came from. Did it herself and was too frightened to say."

Everyone went out the of room except Frances. Monday sat up and said:

"They don't believe me, do they? None of you believe me."

Frances said nothing and followed the others out of the room. For the rest of the day they nursed little Monday and she became strong again, but nobody said much to her. She had fought bravely against the fire, but everyone thought she had started it. Nobody believed the story of the two men and the tin of oil.

4

Next morning, when the baker's wife went in to see Monday, she had gone. The bed was untidy, and some of Frances' clothes were missing. Monday was nowhere to be found.

"Oh well," said the baker's wife. "She'll turn up like a bad ha'penny, when she's least expected. Meanwhile, there's one less breakfast to cook."

But Monday didn't turn up. Instead, half way through the morning, two policemen came on bicycles.

They told the baker that two rough-looking men had been caught the night before trying to burn down another bakery in a town some ten miles away. So it looked as if little Monday's story was true after all. Yes, said the policemen, they had owned up to trying to burn down the baker's bakehouse the night before that. Now the baker and his family began to be sorry that Monday had gone. She had been a naughty little trouble-maker, but she had evidently not done so dreadful a thing as burn down a house. They questioned the police about her, but nothing was known. The police promised to look out for her and make enquiries.

Days and weeks passed, but still Monday did not come back. The bakehouse was re-built out of the money that the baker had saved, and after a few months they had all settled down peacefully, and life was much the same as it had been before they had ever set eyes on Monday. The new bakehouse was better and more up-to-date than the old one had been, and soon the baker was doing well and making up for the business he had lost during the weeks when he had been able to do no baking.

Tom got to the top of his class, and Frances kept her dolls as neat and tidy as ever. Their mother went on with her sewing and cooking and cleaning, and never made any more unkind remarks about the baker's pipe.

But something was missing. They could never be quite as happy as they had been in the days before little Monday had come and dripped on the hearth-rug. The neighbours did not gossip over the wall with the baker's wife, because there was not so much to gossip about. There was no Monday to grumble at, for the stories of her misdeeds had always been something to talk about. True, there were fewer cups broken, and fewer balls of wool were tangled up, and Tom's toys were not left out at night and Frances' pinafore was not covered with mud. All the same, something was missing.

"It's not the same without her," said Frances.

"It certainly isn't," said Tom. "No more broken dolls."

"No more singing," said Frances.

"That's right," said Tom. "I used to like the singing. I wonder why father doesn't sing now."

"She was rather horrid, you know."

"Yes. All the same, I sometimes wish she was back."

Then one Sunday they all went out to tea with an aunt who lived several streets away. When they came back, it was dark. The baker went to the table in the middle of the room where the lamp always stood. As he felt in his pocket for matches, he heard a faint purring sound. He lit the lamp. When the flame had burnt up, he saw, sitting on the table, an ugly grey cat with one ear. It bounded down from the table and rubbed itself against his leg.

"Hallo," said the baker, "where have I seen you before?"

"Hallo," said his wife, "who's been at my knitting? I'm sure I left it tidy when we went out."

"Hallo," said Tom, "who's been using my paint-box and got all the colours mixed up?

"Hallo," said Frances, "where's my best doll gone? I'm sure I left her sitting in the armchair."

"Somebody's been here," said the baker's wife. "I told you we ought to have locked the front door."

"It's that girl," said the baker. "And I did lock the

front door. She'd get in anywhere, that young scally-wag."

But Monday was nowhere to be found. They looked in the kitchen and the yard and the bakehouse, and there was not a sign of her. The baker's wife took a candle and went upstairs to put away her best coat and hat. A moment later she came to the top of the stairs and said:

"Come upstairs, all of you, and bring the lamp. I've something to show you."

They all went up to the big bedroom. There fast asleep in the middle of the bed, and tucked up in the clean eiderdown, was a ragged, grubby little girl with black hair and a wide grinning mouth. Clutched in her grimy arms was Frances' best doll.

The baker and his wife and Tom and Frances stood round the bed in silence, not daring to wake her.

"I wonder if she's come for always this time," said Frances.

The baker's wife sighed and turned to her husband.

"I wish she could sleep like that all the time," she said, "even in my best eiderdown."

Then the little girl in bed turned in her sleep and smiled, showing all her teeth.

"Come on, children," said the baker quietly. "Best come downstairs and get supper."

"And hurry off to bed," said their mother. "Monday tomorrow."

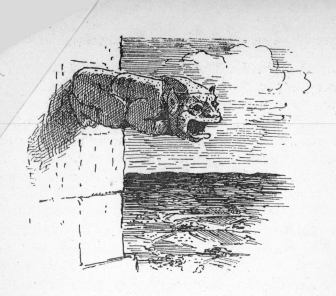

The Stonemason of Elphinstone

I

THIS is a story about the village of Elphinstone, and how it got its name. The village is not the one in Scotland, but another of the same name in one of the northern counties of England. In the centre of the village stands a church, with a great stone tower. If you look up at the top of the tower, you will see that at each corner is a gargoyle—that is, a strange figure carved in stone leaning out so that the rain which falls on the roof of the tower may trickle out of the creature's mouth on to the ground below. The four gargoyles at the top of Elphinstone tower are all different, and one of them is very strange indeed. But let us start the story at the beginning, which is the proper place to start, after all.

Many years ago—it might have been five hundred

and it might have been more—there was a knight living in the north country called Sir John Tilbury. Now he was getting old, and he had made a great deal of money by the sale of wool, and he thought he would like to do something with his money so that people would remember him after he died. He decided to build a church. On the edge of his land there were many poor people living, and they had no church to go to nearer than ten miles. It would be a good thing, thought Sir John, if they had a church of their own; so he had plans made, and hired workmen —carpenters, labourers and masons. The work went well, and before many years passed, the church was nearly finished. It was a fine, tall building of grey stone with richly carved window-frames and a great square tower at the western end. The carpenters had put in the roof-timbers and the glaziers had even put some of the glass into the windows. Before long only a few finishing touches remained to be done.

Now one of the stonemasons at work on the church was a man named Martin. He was getting on for middle-age, not very tall and with curly brown hair; his work in the open air had made his skin brown and weather-beaten, and his clothes and his hair and the wrinkles on his face were all filled with the dust of his trade. He was a good mason; there was no one better in all the country for squaring and trimming the grey stone blocks and smoothing the surface of them with his iron chisels. What he loved doing above every-thing else was carving stone figures, and oak leaves and vine leaves, and twisted patterns in stone to go round the arches of doors and windows. He had spent his life carving such things, and nobody could do it better than he.

But he had a fault. Few of us are perfect, and Martin was not what we should call a regular workman. Sometimes he would leave his work for a whole day, or even longer, and stay at home, or go wandering on the moors; he would even throw up a job altogether, when it was only half done; or he would toss his mallet and his chisels into a leather bag and make off to the town to sit gossiping with travellers at an inn or a fair-ground. Time and again the master mason in charge of the work on the church would speak to Martin about his bad ways, sometimes he would even complain to Sir John himself, and Sir John would ask the master mason why he did not get rid of Martin and find somebody more reliable.

"Well, to tell you the truth, Sir John," the master mason said, "I can't find another like him for squaring a corner-stone or knocking a saint's head or a bunch of grapes or the devil himself—begging your pardon, Sir John!—out of a lump of stone. So I'm loath to get rid of him, you see. But if your lordship would have a word with him one day, perhaps he'd listen to you. It does seem a pity, sir, that it does, that a mason like him should be such an awkward, unserviceable fellow."

Sir John said he would have a word with Martin next time he saw him at work.

Martin was a widower. His wife had died leaving him one son and one daughter. Together they lived in a little cottage not far from where the church was being built. The boy worked for the blacksmith, and a very regular, trustworthy boy he was—not at all like his father, the people said. The daughter, Alison, was a good-looking, cheerful girl of sixteen years or so, and it was she who kept house for her father and her brother. She made their little cottage as neat and clean as a choir-boy on Sunday; she fed the hens, milked the cow, mended the clothes, cooked, washed, and did everything as if she had been a wife and mother herself. Sometimes she had to scold her father for coming in late for supper, or for staying out all night on the moors with his dog, but she loved him dearly and would not have made him unhappy for any thing in the world.

Well one evening Martin came home with a face as long and solemn as a sermon. He found Alison getting the supper ready.

"It's all up with me now," said he. "We're ruined, my dear, and no mistake."

"Whatever's happened, father?" asked his daughter. "Have you been dismissed from your work or what?"

"Not yet. But I shall be soon enough. It's no good, my love; I can't stick at a job and that's all there is about it. Never could. I'm so behindhand with my work that Sir John spoke to me about it himself today."

"Sir John Tilbury?"

"Yes, Sir John himself, that's paying for the new church with the gold he got from selling wool to the Flemings across the sea. Over the moor he came on his white horse, with his old white beard fluttering in the wind like a pinafore on a clothes-line. I could have carved him out of stone for Herod the Great or King Alfred himself, so noble and fine he looked. Straight up to me he comes, just where I stood, chipping away at Saint Peter with his shepherd's crook that's to go over the door to the south porch when I get him finished."

"And what did he say?" asked Alison impatiently.

"Well, to cut a long story short, my dear," answered her father, "he said I was working too slow and I must finish by Hallowe'en or he'd push me out."

"Hallowe'en!" said Alison. "Why, that's not for another six weeks. How much is there left to do?"

"Let's see," said Martin. "When I've finished Saint Peter with his shepherd's crook, there's the battlements round the top of the tower and the four gargoyles at the four corners. I think that's about all."

"That's not so bad," said Alison. "Just you get to bed early, go to work as soon as it's light, and don't go gadding off to the town, and you'll finish it in good time."

"It's easy enough for you to say that!" exclaimed Martin. "Carving stone isn't like making pastry-pies, my girl. There's a tidy lot left to do. Unless the fairies, or Merlin the wizard, or Old Nick himself gives me a hand, I don't know how I shall get it done, and that's the truth."

"For shame, father!" said Alison. "That's no way to talk. Now just you shake that dust from your clothes and wash your face and hands and by that time supper will be ready. It's something you like, too, so don't be long. I can't make pies the same as you carve saints, I know, but I don't waste so much time about it. Cheer up, now, there's a good father."

Presently the boy came in, and they all sat down to supper. Early to bed went Martin, determined to make an early start at the church.

2

At first things went fairly well. Martin went regularly to work, and for hours he would do nothing but chip away at the blocks of stone, scraping and smoothing; then he would climb the wooden scaffolding to the top of the tower and fix the blocks in position. The master mason was pleased with his progress, and pleased too that he had thought of asking Sir John to have a word with Martin. On wet days, when it was impossible to work outside, Martin would sit inside the almost finished church carving away at one of the four gargoyles that were to be placed at the corners of the tower. It was in the form of a long-necked dog with fierce eyes and jaws wide open to let the water pour through. With great care Martin carved the two rows of sharp teeth and the curved, pointed tongue. What a fine carver he was, thought the master mason, and what a good thing it was that he was working so steadily.

Then, when the stone dog was finished, and there were still three weeks left before Hallowe'en—which, you remember, was the date set for finishing the work —Martin felt it was time he had a day off. So calling to his dog to follow, he strode away over the moors to the town. There he fell in with some companions, and together they spent the day chatting and laughing and telling stories.

It was late when he got home that evening, and next day he again did not feel like work.

"What's a man for?" he asked himself, "if he has to work every blessed moment of the day scratching and scraping at lumps of stone?"

So once more he set off with his dog, this time to a fair some miles distant, where there were jugglers and wrestlers to be seen, and ballad-singers to hear.

That evening when he got home, his daughter scolded him.

"That's the second day you've not been to the church, father," she said. "What's to become of us when you are thrown out of work, I should like to know?"

"I'll not be thrown out of work," said Martin. "The job's nearly finished I tell you, and there's near three weeks left. Why, I could finish it in time if I had but one hand!"

"Well, get your supper now," she said, "and off to bed with you, for you must start early in the morning if you're to make up for lost time."

"Lost time!" repeated her father scornfully. "If a man can't take time off once in a way, he might as well be a Hebrew slave working for Pharaoh of Egypt. Besides, the job's nearly finished, I tell you!"

But it was not nearly finished, and he knew it. The

battlements round the tower were only half done, and there were three more gargoyles to be carved and set in place.

Now one of Martin's favourite sports was poaching. He did not often do it, but sometimes when the night was fine and not too cold, and there was a moon shining, the wish to go wandering out of doors came strong upon him. It was forbidden to catch hares and rabbits and birds on Sir John Tilbury's land, but most of the men in the village went out now and again and caught a rabbit for the pot, and no one thought much harm of it.

One of the favourite haunts of poachers was a place called Ferry Hill, which belonged to Sir John. Now the name means 'Fairy Hill', for it is covered with trees and in the centre of the trees is a great mound, under which the country people in those days believed the fairies lived.

Well, one night, when his son and daughter were safely asleep, Martin took a thick stick and a sack and set off for Ferry Hill to see what luck he might have. The moon was full, and although there was a touch of frost in the air, it was not too cold for a night's sport.

Over the fields he went and up the hill. The moon, shining through the trees, made ghostly shadows, but nothing stirred. Not even an owl was abroad, and there was no sound except the cracking of twigs and the rustle of fallen leaves under Martin's feet.

For a time he sat down on his sack and waited. Then he began to think of the work that he still had to do at the church, and he pictured the face of Sir John when he found that it was not finished in time. What would Sir John think, Martin wondered, if he knew that one of his stonemasons was even now trespassing on his land in the hope of catching a rabbit?

"Not much stirring tonight," he said to himself. "I'll just go up to the top of the hill; then if I see nothing, I'll be off home."

So he got up, threw the sack over his shoulder, and made for the green mound in the centre of the wood.

Suddenly he stopped.

"Hallo!" he said. "Now what's that? Rabbit holes, I do believe."

There, just below a grassy bank with brambles growing over it, were two or three round openings, like the entrances to little caves.

Martin bent down. It seemed as if he could hear movements inside the rabbit hole. Quickly he opened his sack and put the mouth of it over the largest hole.

"Now," said the mason, "may Saint Martin, who is my very own patron saint, send him out of his hole and into my sack!"

Even as he spoke, there was a scuffling sound inside the hole and something ran out of it right into the open sack. It kicked and struggled, but Martin, without waiting to look inside, closed the mouth of the sack and tied it into a knot. Then he threw it over his shoulder, picked up his cudgel and made off down the hill.

"A rabbit, I'll be bound," said Martin. "A nice fat rabbit, by the feel of him. And there's nobody can make a rabbit stew like my Alison!"

It was not long before he was back at his own cottage door.

Softly he lifted the latch and went in. There was not a sound to be heard. Son and daughter must be fast asleep. He put the sack on the floor and sat down on the bench beside the table, Without stopping to light a candle, for the full moon sent its light streaming through the window so that it was almost as bright as day, Martin untied the neck of the sack. But first he looked round to see that the door was shut, so that the rabbit could not escape.

Instantly there was a scurrying of limbs inside the sack and out ran—*not* a furry grey rabbit, but a two-legged creature dressed in brown, with the face of an old man! His little black eyes glittered in the moon-light. He wore a pointed cap of brown leather, and he stood about as high as the length of your fore-arm from the wrist to the elbow. He sprang first on the table and stood with his hands on his hips.

Martin had nearly shouted out in surprise at seeing the little man, but he managed to keep quiet for fear of waking his son and daughter. When he had recovered from his surprise, he said politely:

"Good evening to you. Who are you and what's your name?"

The little man answered him in rhyme.

"Who am I and what's my name?
No man on earth can tell this same.
If ever my name on earth is known,
This same elf shall turn to stone."

"That wouldn't do at all," said Martin. "But truth to say, I mistook you for a rabbit. I've no wish to go catching elves and fairies and such as you. I'll give you a shilling for your trouble, and you can be off home."

"A shilling!" said the elf scornfully. "Never offer me and my likes money! But if you'll give me some white bread and a bowl of milk, perhaps I can help you."

"I'll give you the bread and the milk willingly," said Martin, "but as for helping me, I doubt if there's anything a little fellow like you can do."

"There's nothing I *can't* do," said the elf. "You're in trouble, aren't you? You're a stonemason, aren't you, and you've work to finish by Hallowe'en that you can't get done in time, eh?"

"I must have been talking to myself," answered Martin, "and you must have overheard me."

"Perhaps I didn't, perhaps I did. Well, luckily for you, I'm a stone worker myself. I can build bridges and make roads. I don't care for church work greatly, for the parsons say hard things about me and my kind, but seeing you're in trouble I'll give you a hand."

"It's very kind of you," Martin began, but the elf went on.

"Now if I help you to finish your work by Hallowe'en you must do something for me. Do you hear?"

"And what's that?" said Martin, smiling. He could not help thinking what a strange business it was to be making a bargain with such an odd little creature.

"You must give me your daughter to marry," said the elf.

"What, my daughter Alison?" asked Martin, hardly believing his ears.

"And why not?" said the elf. "She's a decent lass, for I've seen her about the countryside. Ah yes, I've seen her when she couldn't see me. She'll do well enough."

Martin hesitated.

"Well, what do you say?" went on the elf. "If I help you finish off your work on the new church, will you

108

give me your daughter to marry on Hallowe'en day? Is it a bargain?"

"What if she should refuse?" said Martin. "She's very particular. She might not fancy being wed to such a little fellow as yourself."

And then, seeing the elf looking angry, he went on:

"That is, I don't think she's a mind to get married at all just now. What shall I do if she says no?"

"If you make a bargain with me," answered the elf, "you must stick to it. There's only one way you can get out of it, though it's scarcely worth the telling."

"And what's that?"

"If you can guess my name, you can keep your daughter, and you'll never see me alive again."

Martin said nothing. He got up and went to the larder, bringing out white bread and a bowl of creamy milk.

"Here," he said, "have this while I think a bit."

And as the elf ate the bread and drank the milk, Martin walked up and down the room thinking. How could he make such a bargain? How could he promise his only daughter to such a comical, wizened old fellow? And how would Alison fancy a husband no bigger than her fore-arm? But then, what a help it would be to have the work finished in time! There was barely a week left, and there was no other way of getting it done.

"Perhaps I'm dreaming," thought Martin. "Perhaps he can't help me at all. Ah well, why shouldn't I let him have a try? If he *does* manage to do the work for me, there'll be some way out of letting him wed Alison. After all, it shouldn't be such a difficult matter to find out his name. If the worst comes to the worst, I can go and tell the schoolmaster or the priest, and they'll know for sure, with all their deep learning and their books and such stuff. I'll do it."

So he made the bargain with the elf, and when he had done so he felt a great weight off his mind. The little man's dark eyes twinkled and he smiled a crafty smile as he hopped down off the table.

"Now mind," he said, "I'm a man of my word. See that you stick to yours!"

"Never fear, I will," answered Martin and opened the door quietly.

Before there was time to wish the elf goodnight, he had scurried out of the door and disappeared in the darkness. For by now the moon had almost set.

Martin laughed to himself at his odd adventure. Then he yawned and went to bed.

3

Next morning the sun was shining brightly by the time Martin woke up. His daughter was knocking on the door and telling him to hurry and get dressed or he would have cold porridge. So Martin got up, and after breakfast he set off for the church.

What was his surprise to find, neatly piled up waiting for him, ten or a dozen perfectly carved stone blocks! He had certainly not done them himself the day before, and no one else could have carved them except the elf.

"Well I never," thought Martin. "So he's going to help me after all. A very clever workman he is too, and no mistake. I couldn't have squared those blocks better myself."

He took one of the new blocks under one arm and hoisted himself up the scaffolding to the top of the tower. The block exactly fitted the place where it had to go. Leaving it there, Martin went down and mixed some mortar to set the stone hard and keep it in position.

Before long he had cemented all the blocks in place and begun to carve a new one. Then a thought struck him.

"If the little fellow's going to do all the plain stones." he said to himself, "why should I trouble myself about them? I'll get on with the figures."

So he began to shape a piece of stone for the corner of the tower, on which he could carve the second gargoyle. The first had been a fierce dog-like creature with sharp teeth and his tongue hanging out. The next was to be a bird, a long-necked eagle with out-

spread wings. All the rest of that day Martin worked
on the eagle and at sundown he went off home to his
cottage.

When he saw his dear daughter Alison making up
the fire and beginning to get the supper ready, he
suddenly felt sorry for his bargain. What if, after all,
the dwarf should really claim her as his bride and
carry her off to live in his dark hole under the Ferry
Hill? Perhaps he should tell her all about it, and ask
her pardon, and then go off to the hill in search of the
elf and tell him the bargain was off. He ought never
to have meddled with such matters.

Then he thought to himself: "But if this is an evil
business, why did I catch the little scamp just as I was
in need of help? Was he not sent to me in my time of
need? What have I to be afraid of? Time to start
fretting when Hallowe'en comes."

He thought no more of the matter and set about
cleaning the dust out of his curly hair and getting
ready for the good food Alison was preparing.

Next day it was the same. A neat pile of beautifully
carved stones was waiting for Martin when he got to
the church. Once again he climbed the scaffolding to
the top of the high tower and fixed them in place
next to the ones he had cemented in the day before.
Then he went on with his stone eagle, and so well
did he work that by the end of the day he had
finished it.

Each day it was the same, and when the master
mason came to see how he was doing, he was delighted
with Martin's progress.

"Why," he said, "now if you'd only work like this
all the time, you could be a master mason yourself
and have fifty men working for you. And to think

you've done all this by yourself! Anyone would think you had evil spirits working for you!"

"Evil spirits don't make good masons," said Martin, scowling at his master.

"I daresay they don't," answered the master mason. "Well, you've three more days, and it looks as if you'll have no trouble to finish the job in time. Good luck to you!"

Next day Martin finished the third gargoyle, and fitted it to the corner where he had left a space for it between the stones shaped by the elf. It was a strange creature, something like a fish, with broad curved fins and wide open mouth.

On the day before Hallowe'en he got to work as usual, and as usual he found the newly squared blocks all ready for him. When he had cemented these in position, he found that only two were still lacking—two blocks and one figure. The work would easily be done in time, that is, if the elf was as good as his word. So he sat down and began to consider what form the fourth gargoyle should take. Perhaps it should be a little demon, he thought. But Sir John might not like that. Perhaps it should be a little dwarf with pointed ears and a crafty smile. But this might offend the elf who had been helping him all this time. So in the end he decided that the last figure should be a dragon. Yes, that was it—a long-necked dragon with a crest over its head, curling teeth, sharp claws, and scales all down its neck. That would remind people of the dragon that Saint George had killed, and nobody could possibly be offended. So without more hesitation, he chose a suitable piece of stone and began chipping away.

He had half finished the figure when the day began

to fade and it was almost time to pack up his tools and set off for home.

All at once there was a little scuffling noise and he turned round to find the elf standing behind him.

"Hallo," exclaimed the mason, "how you scared me! Where have you been all this time?"

> "Whence I come and Whither I go,
>   All may guess but none may know,"

answered the elf.

"Well, you're a neat enough stone-worker," said Martin, "if it's you that's been shaping these stone blocks for me."

"It's me all right," said the elf. "Who else, I should like to know? We shall finish the job tomorrow, you and I, and then—then I shall come for my fee. This time tomorrow I'll be with you—an hour before sundown, do you hear?"

"I hear," said the mason. "But it's not tomorrow yet. It'll be time enough to claim your fee when the work's done."

The elf chuckled.

"Well," he said. "I just stepped along to remind you of the day. I'll be here tomorrow, never fear. And mind—no tricks."

Before Martin could answer, the little man had scurried off as fast as he had come, and in two seconds not a sign of him was to be seen.

Martin packed up his tools and made off home with a heavy heart.

That night he hardly slept at all. He tossed and turned on his bed, and his mind was torn with nightmares. He thought he saw a fearsome creature

coming for him with the body of a dragon and the face
of the little dwarf, and just as it was about to reach
him, he woke up, trembling with fright.

At last the morning came. It was Hallowe'en, the
day when the work was to be finished, the day when
he was to pay the price for all his idleness and folly.

When he got to the church he found the last two
blocks of stone waiting for him, just as he knew they
would be. He had half hoped the elf might have
forgotten to do his share of the work, so that the
bargain would be broken. But there they were,
neatly squared and smoothed, as the others had been.
Slowly he climbed the scaffolding with one of them
under his arm. It seemed to him as heavy as lead. It
fitted perfectly, and so did the other. Before the
morning was half through, he had fixed them both in
place and begun work on the dragon that was to fill
up the last space at the top of the tower.

As Martin cut and scraped, the day wore on. At
last, fully half an hour before the time when the elf
had promised to come, the figure was finished. There
it was, all ready to cement into place. But Martin had
not the heart to carry it to the top of the tower. Instead he sat down on a pile of stones and began
brooding on what was to come. Should he run away?
Should he pretend not to see the elf when he came?
Should he strike at him with his hammer or chase him
away with stones?

While he was thinking these thoughts, a man came
up to him. It was Peter, an old carpenter who had
been working with him on the church some time
before. He was one of the men who had put in the
great beams which supported the roof. Martin did
not like him, for he was a hard man to deal with, and

at times he was cross-grained and rough in his manner. But just now he seemed in a good humour.

"Why, Martin," said Peter, "you've a face as long as a handsaw! Can't you get the work finished in time? I did hear as you was to finish by today or Sir John was going to throw you out."

"The work's finished," said Martin, "or as good as finished. As for being thrown out of work, I care not whether I am or not."

"What have you been a-shaping there?" went on Peter. "Why, I shouldn't wonder it if was your own dragon that's put you out of temper, for it's as life-like and fearsome a dragon as ever I saw! Now that would be a fine thing to scare away evil spirits. I should like to have a figure like that to fix over my door! Then my old woman wouldn't be so mortal scared of demons as she is. But I tell you what, Martin. You've been working too hard. What you need is a night's sport. What do you say to coming out with me next full moon, and scaring up a few of Sir John's birds or perhaps a rabbit or two?"

"Perhaps I will and perhaps I won't," said Martin.

"Only there's one place I won't go," Peter continued, "and that's Ferry Hill. I tell you, there's spirits round there. Some folks don't believe in them, but I know better. I'll tell you something I saw last night, though you won't believe me."

"And what's that?" asked Martin.

"Well, I was a-coming home late, because I'd been over to the Hall to tighten up a pair of shutters that had shaken loose in the wind. I was coming home late and I passed by the stone quarry on the other side of Ferry Hill. And what should I see—it was getting dark, you understand, and I couldn't make out nothing plain, but——"

"Yes, what did you see?" said Martin impatiently.

"You'll not believe me, but I tell you, dark as it was, I saw a little fellow no longer than my smoothing plane, standing up beside a great block of stone, a-chipping and a-chopping with a little silver chisel and a mallet! Ah, you may laugh, Martin, but I tell you it was one of them dwarfs or spirits or such-like that lives under Ferry Hill. And while he was a-working, he was singing to himself."

"Did you hear what he sang?" asked Martin.

"I did that," said Peter. "He had a little high, quavery voice, and what he sang went something like this. Let me see. 'Something or other is my name;' no, that's not it.

'Something or other's the name of this same elf.
Nobody knows it but myself.

If ever my name on earth is known,
This same elf shall turn to stone.' "

Martin had suddenly become excited.

"What did he say his name was?" he asked eagerly.

"Why that I can't remember," said Peter, "for it meant nothing to me."

"But you *must* remember!" said Martin. "Think, think!"

"I can't remember," repeated the carpenter. "What's it to you anyhow?"

"Never mind," said Martin. "If you can remember what the little fellow's name was, I'll give you anything you want!"

"Well, I *might* call it to mind," said Peter, "if I was to think hard enough. But what'll you give me if I think of it, eh? You wouldn't give me that stone dragon you've been a-making now, would you?"

Martin hesitated. If he promised Peter the dragon, how could he make another before the night was out? But what did that matter if only he could find out the elf's name? For he was certain that the little man Peter had seen working in the stone quarry was no other than the very same elf who had been helping him.

"Done!" he cried. "If you can tell me what the dwarf said, you shall have the gargoyle. There! Now think hard!"

"Give me time," answered Peter. "Let me see. 'Something's the name of this same elf, Nobody knows it but myself'. It's a fine figure of a dragon, that! It'll look terrible fierce over my door, it will. Now what *did* the little fellow say his name was?"

"Oh hurry!" said Martin, for the sun was beginning to go down and the shadows were lengthening.

Peter scratched his head and knocked on it with his knuckles. At last he said:

"I've got it—I've got it! 'Lob is the name of this same elf.'—No, that's not it neither. But it was something very like. 'Cob' or 'Hob', may be. 'Nob'! That's it! 'Nob is the name of this same elf. Nobody knows it but myself.' That's what the little fellow sang. I can hear him now with his chip-chip-chip on the stone and his little high voice——"

He was interrupted by a distant rumble of thunder.

"Hallo," he said, "storm coming up. I'd best be a-getting home. That was the name all right, so if you're satisfied I'll just take up my fee in this bag and be off with me."

"Take it, take it!" said Martin, full of joy. He picked up the stone dragon which, though heavy, could easily be carried by a strong man, and gave it to the carpenter.

Peter thanked him, opened his carpenter's bag on the ground and placed the figure safely inside. Then he hoisted it on his shoulder, bade Martin goodnight and made off.

"Perhaps Sir John will give me two days extra to make another," said Martin to himself. "What do I care, so long as I get out of my cursed bargain? And if that fellow Peter has told me wrong, I'll go and fetch the dragon back myself."

No sooner had he spoken than there was another rumble of thunder, louder than the first, and the sun was darkened by a great cloud. Standing beside Martin was the elf. He hopped on to a block of stone and looked at the mason with his black, glittering eyes.

"Here I am," he said, "an hour before sundown, just as I said. Perhaps you thought I wouldn't come?"

Martin said nothing.

"But I've come all right," the elf went on. "Have I helped with the work as I said, and is it finished in time?"

"Yes," said Martin, "you've helped as you promised, and the work is done."

"And now for my wages! Are you going to give me my bride, as you agreed, or must I go and take her?"

And the elf chuckled and pointed in the direction of the village.

"No!" shouted Martin. "I'll not give you my daughter, and you'll not take her! Get you gone where you came from, Master NOB—and never let me see you again! Do you hear—Master NOB?"

At the sound of his name the elf screamed horribly, and leaned out across the stone he was standing on. He waved his fist at Martin, and with an expression of hatred and malice on his little wizened face, he opened his mouth as if to spit poison. As he did so, there was a flash of lightning, a loud peal of thunder, and Martin fell senseless to the ground.

Then the thunder-storm passed, and Martin came to himself, his face and hands splashed with rain. There in front of him, as if carved in stone, was the figure of the elf just as Martin had last seen him, his mouth open and his face twisted with rage. Then he thought of the words of the elf's song:

"If ever my name on earth is known,
This same elf shall turn to stone."

In what was left of the daylight, Martin saw that

the elf, turned to stone, was now part of the block on which he had been standing. It was the very same size as that on which he had carved the dragon. Now he had another gargoyle instead—a very different one! Instead of the scaly dragon with a crest and sharp claws, there was the figure of a little, evil-faced dwarf with pointed cap and open mouth.

"That'll scare away the evil spirits," said Martin to himself as he carried the figure to the top of the tower. It fitted exactly. Quickly he cemented the gargoyle in its place, put a sack over it so that the mortar would not spoil with the rain, and went off home in the gathering darkness.

That is the story which is told of the fourth gargoyle on the tower of Elphinstone Church. And when Sir John Tilbury, the old, rich merchant, saw Martin's handiwork, he was especially struck by the figure of the elf.

"Why," said he, "the village shall be named after that same carving, for I never saw so good a one before. It shall be called 'Elf-in-Stone', for that's what all travellers to this place will see when they raise their heads to the tower —an Elf in stone."

In this way Martin the mason kept both his daughter and his job, and the village where he lived got a new church and a new name.

About the author
James Reeves was born in 1909 near London and began his career as a poet. Soon he was writing stories and poems especially for children, and in 1950 his first collection of children's poetry, *The Wandering Moon*, was published. James Reeves' fascination with folklore and mythology is reflected in many of his works including this volume.

About the artist
Edward Ardizzone has built up a reputation as a top-class illustrator over many years. He is particularly well known for his books about Tim's adventures at sea, which he wrote and illustrated between 1936 and 1972. The volume which appeared in 1956, *Tim All Alone*, won the first Kate Greenaway medal. Ardizzone's close collaboration with the authors whose work he portrays has been particularly successful in the case of James Reeves, the element of nostalgia in the artist's work being a perfect complement to the writer's tales of magic and legend.

More Beaver Books

We hope you have enjoyed this Beaver Book. Here are some of the other titles:

Plot Night John and his friends plan a huge bonfire for Plot Night, but at the last moment things go wrong. By William Mayne

The Tail of the Trinosaur Charles Causley's splendidly funny verse story about a prehistoric beast which comes to England from the Amazon jungle, with illustrations by Jill Gardiner

My Favourite Animal Stories Sad, funny and exciting stories about all sorts of animals, chosen and introduced by Gerald Durrell

All the Fun of the Fair When the fair comes to town, Kay, Rory and Gerald have amusing adventures with a fortune-teller, a lady bareback rider, the elephant boy and the baby elephant who loves apples; written by Dorothy Clewes for younger readers

Rebecca's World Written by Terry Nation of Daleks fame, with illustrations by Larry Learmonth, this is a rich and comic fantasy with a memorable cast of characters

Lord of the Forest Written by 'BB' and with beautiful illustrations by Denys Watkins-Pitchford, this is the story of a mighty oak from its planting in 1272 until the last acorn from the dead tree is replanted in the 1939–45 war. A magnificent panorama of nature and history

New Beavers are published every month and if you would like the *Beaver Bulletin* – which gives all the details – please send a stamped addressed envelope to:

Beaver Bulletin
The Hamlyn Group
Astronaut House
Hounslow Road
Feltham
Middlesex TW14 9AR

371336

Snail Tale by Avi

Avon the Snail believes that you can't be really happy until you've had adventures, so one day he sets off with Edward the Ant to look for some. The two friends find plenty on their travels to the end of the branch and back, and Avon gets the chance to fight a famous battle and do a very brave deed. The author and illustrator both come from New Jersey, where Avi lectures in children's literature at Trenton State College.

The Tail of the Trinosaur by Charles Causley
For ninety million years (or thereabouts) a TRINOSAUR has lain undisturbed in the clay of the Amazon Jungle. But when this fantastic creature is finally unearthed and sent as a gift to the peace-loving township of Dunborough, then it becomes very disturbed indeed.

The effect for Dunborough's good citizens is shattering. For the reader, the outcome is a hilarious story in rhyme by one of Britain's foremost poets that is sheer delight from beginning to end.

Jill Gardiner's zany illustrations add to the fun and help to make Charles Causley's first-ever story for children a unique and special book.